WARNING

Due to the explicit language and graphic sexual scenes, this book is intended for mature (18 years +) readers only.

If things of this nature offend you, this book would not be for you. If you like a good, steamy romance with tiger shifters, then you have chosen wisely...

--Ariel Marie

CHAPTER ONE

Deja crept back to her bed as slow as she could. She sent up a prayer that she could make it to the plush mattress, where she could potentially get at least one more hour of sleep. Her eyes were heavy and begged to shut. She took another step and reached her hand out.

Almost there.

The wood floor was usually unforgiving, but tonight, the big guy upstairs was looking out for her. She leapt and landed softly on the bed, then quickly crawled underneath her comforter as she tried to hide from the chilled air. She held her breath and peeked from beneath her cover and stared out across her small bedroom.

Quiet.

She sighed as she rolled over onto her side, and tucked her pillow beneath her head.

"Thank goodness," she whispered.

Her three-month-old son, Augie, was still asleep. August Dixon Scarlett was her pride and joy. Right now, the little stinker had yet to master the art of sleeping through the night.

If she weren't so tired she would laugh at herself. Life as a single mother to a three-month-old was certainly not glamorous, but she wouldn't trade it for all the money in the world.

But she knew that one day it would come. She just had to hold out and continue working with him to finally get her much-needed, sleep-filled nights.

She peeked over at the small crib again and took in his still form. He was her angel, her everything.

She wished she didn't have to do the single mom thing, but it was what it was. There was no way that she could contact his father and tell him that he had left her a little present.

She sighed.

His father.

There wasn't a day that went by that she didn't think of Dixon. He was her tall, dark, and handsome that she had met a year ago while working as a waitress at the Ski Bar and Grille. The minute their eyes had met, her body reacted to his like no other man before. He and his friends had kept her laughing all night while she served them, but it was him that she had eyes for, and he for her.

Dixon, as all other patrons of the Ski Bar and Grille, had come to Breckenridge for the fun, snow, and skiing. He had come into the bar a total of three times, always requesting to be seated in her section. By the last time, he had won her over with his intense amber eyes. Just remembering his heated look had her squeezing her legs shut.

How could a memory of a single look make her want him all over again?

She already knew the answer.

Their single night together was one that she would never forget. He had taken care of her sexually in such a way that she couldn't even remember her past lover's names. He had totally ruined her for the next man. Whoever she would have a relationship with in the future would have big shoes—very big shoes—to fill.

Just the thought of how her softer body felt against his hard, naked one sent a shiver down her spine. That night she had been able to trace every ridge of muscle on his abdomen with her tongue. It had been a magical night. She could remember it as if it were yesterday. The memory of his thick length filling her, thrusting deep inside of her, caused her breath to catch. She groaned as her core clenched. That single night had left her a small gift that she would forever hold dear to her heart.

A small cry filled the air.

Augie.

She paused, waiting to see if he would calm down, but the cry grew louder. She turned over and looked at her alarm clock and rolled her eyes. There was no point in staying in the bed.

"Okay, Mommy's coming," she announced, flinging back the covers and standing from the bed. There wasn't much room in her bedroom, aside from her and Augie's bed. She rented a one bedroom, one bathroom apartment at the base of the Rocky Mountains. The area wasn't the best, but it wasn't rundown. It was what she could afford on a waitress' salary at the moment.

"It's all right. I'm here," she cooed as she reached into the crib and picked him up. He immediately calmed down as she cradled him to her. She gave up on the notion of sleep and carried him over to her bed. Turning on the light, she placed him on the bed. "Now why can't Momma's little man just sleep through the night?"

A smile spread across his little face and her heart melted. He looked just like Dixon, with those same dark hair and amber eyes. She didn't know Dixon's last name, or even how to get a hold of him. She knew deep down that she should inform him that he had become a father, but shame washed over her.

What if he was married and had a family already? What if she was just a one-night stand while away with the guys? Would he even want to see her again? Would he even want to know about Augie?

She smiled at her little man as she checked his diaper. She loved his name, August. It came to her in a dream and she knew it would fit him perfectly. She gave him his father's first name as a middle name, just so he could have some part of his father as he grew up in life. She knew that when he grew up she would have to explain his father's absence, and she dreaded that day.

I'm sorry, son. Your mother had a one-night stand, and I never caught your father's last name.

She bit her lip as tears blurred her vision, but she willed them back, not wanting to cry. She'd done enough of that when she found out she was pregnant. She was an only child, and her parents were both deceased.

It was just she and Augie.

Her little gift that she received on a steamy Christmas morning.

Thank goodness for her best friend, Niki Vincent, and her babysitter, Sharon Hickman. She didn't know what she would do without the two of them. Niki had recently been trying to convince Deja to move to Colorado Springs with her, and lately, Deja had been thinking on it. It would be nice to share some of these late-night sessions with someone.

"Okay, August Dixon Scarlett. You're up, I'm up, so we might as well get this day started."

Dixon stared across the desk at his best friend, Percy Sinnett. They had been best friends since they were cubs, and right now, his friend stared at him as if he grew another head.

"What's wrong with that? We had a really good time last year," Dixon said, tapping his fingers along the sturdy mahogany wood.

"It's just that we usually don't have the council meeting in the same town two years in a row," Percy replied, settling back in his chair.

Dixon's tiger huffed. His friend was right, but Dixon had an alternative reason for why he wanted to go back to the Rocky Mountains. His animal loved running around in the thick forest in the midst of all the snow. As a tiger shifter, he needed to be able to let his animal roam free, and his tiger loved to run through the snow in the winter.

But there was another reason that Dixon wanted to go back to Breckenridge, Colorado.

Deja.

The sexy waitress that had plagued his mind and dreams for the past year. He had contemplated going back to see her, but didn't want to seem like a stalker. They'd had one night together that he couldn't shake from his mind. Shit, he didn't even know her last name to even look her up.

How many women in Breckenridge had the first name of Deja? Maybe he could call the bar where she worked and see if they would give him her information.

Hell no, they wouldn't, he scoffed at himself.

This had not been the first time that he'd had a one-night stand. In all of his years he'd had plenty of them, and most he couldn't even remember the women's names, but Deja stood out to him. She, at first, would cross his mind, and his tiger would whine about not being with her anymore. As time drew on, the need to see her grew. He literally ached in his chest to see her.

"What's wrong with doing something out of the ordinary?" he asked, chuckling. He didn't want to let his friend know that he was causing a fuss over a woman. He would never live that down.

"I guess nothing is wrong with it." Percy smiled and released a chuckle. "We did have some fun nights while we were there, and if I recall, you did disappear that last night with the pretty little waitress. I'm sure you don't even remember her name. She was something pretty."

"Deja," he murmured unconsciously. He remembered her name. There was no way he could forget her. His tiger paced beneath his skin at the thought of her clear blue eyes and her thick brunette waves.

"Wow," Percy chuckled, breaking into Dixon's thoughts.

"What?"

"That's why you want to go back to Breckenridge! The little waitress has caught Dixon Blackburn's attention." Percy shook his head as he laughed. Dixon scowled at his friend for knowing him too well. "Have you had any contact with her since we left?"

Dixon shook his head. His scowl grew as his friend laughed harder at his expense. He blew out a deep breath and turned away from his friend. Standing from his office desk, he walked over to the massive window that looked out onto the city. He wondered if she had even thought of him since last year. Did she even remember him?

He had kept this secret to himself until recently, when he turned to his mother with his problem. Amelda Blackburn had listened to him pour his heart out about his regret at leaving Deja behind and never going back. It was his mother who had made him see why his tiger was acting the way he was. She urged him to go back and find Deja.

"I just can't get her out of my mind. Lately, the need to see her has grown stronger. My animal wants to tear out of here and go find her. I think she's my—"

"Mate?" Percy's response caused both of them to pause. Dixon hadn't really said the word out loud before, but the way that his tiger had been acting lately, he knew it to be true. He needed to find her. "It's taken you almost a year to figure that out?"

He snorted at how he and his tiger had almost missed that she was his mate. Mating for a tiger was a once in a lifetime chance. Missing a mate would mean that he would spend an entire lifetime without his other half. His tiger knew it though. That's what it had been trying to tell him, but he just hadn't listened to his animal.

"Yes, I think Deja was my mate and I let her slip through my fingers."

CHAPTER TWO

"The snow is really kicking up," Deja murmured as she glanced out the window. She had returned back to work a week ago. It felt good to have regular conversations with adults. Not that she didn't love Augie, but it was nice to have an actual conversation with someone who could form syllables.

"The weatherman is calling for another foot of snow by midnight," Alana replied as she came to stand next to Deja. They both tried to look out the front window, but the flurries had picked up, causing a whiteout.

"The temperature sure is dropping tonight." Deja shivered from the cold that was seeping through the thick windows.

"Hopefully, they'll close up a little early tonight,"

Alana murmured as they walked toward the bar. "It is the Christmas season."

"Don't hold your breath," Luna, the bartended, snorted. Deja knew that closing early on a Friday was not happening. Not that there was anyone coming into the Ski Bar and Grille that was located on top of a mountain in the middle of a snowstorm.

"She's right, they're not closing tonight." Deja hopped up on the stool and let her feet swing freely. "We might as well wait out the snow. We're not going to be able to get down off the mountain in this."

Deja was a little worried about the ride home. Augie was with his trustful babysitter, Sharon, and she knew he was safe. It had been a Godsend to find Sharon. She began her search for a babysitter when she was pregnant and found it was hard for her to be able to find someone to watch Augie that she trusted. Sharon came highly recommend from Luna, whose sister was neighbors with Sharon.

The minute they met, they had hit it off and became close friends. Sharon was a retired police dispatcher who babysat for her grandchildren and took on Augie. It pleased Deja that Augie would be around a family atmosphere instead of a facility. If she had to think of a facility, she might have quit her job to be able to care for him.

Sharon barely allowed Deja to pay her. Deja had to almost force money into the woman's hand. Sharon refused to take what normal babysitters charged from a single mother.

"Alana, can you cover my table? I want to go and check on Augie," Deja asked, worry filling her chest. If she didn't need the money, she would have just took the day off with the snow rolling in the way it was.

"Sure." Alana strolled over to the table with their only guest in the entire bar. Deja headed toward the back breakroom as she pulled her cell phone from her back pocket to call Sharon.

"Hey, Deja," Sharon answered.

"Hey, Sharon. How's my main man doing?" she asked, leaning up against the wall. She bit her bottom lip, thinking of her little man's chubby cheeks. She smiled as she heard his cooing in the background.

"Oh, he's doing just fine, Deja." Deja could hear Sharon make baby talk to Augie. She smiled as she imagined his smiles.

"That's good. I'm going to try to head out a little early with all this snow coming down."

"You be careful coming down the mountain. You know it's going to take you a lot longer to get here. You know August will be fine spending the night. Safety first, young lady." Sharon's voice became a little stern, as only a mother protecting her child would be. She was a mother figure to Deja, which caused her heart to warm. She missed her own mother dearly. Sharon reminded her of Sylvia Scarlett.

Tears welled up in Deja's eyes at the thought of her deceased parents. She wished that her mother was here to meet her grandchild. Sylvia would have just loved Augie. His amber eyes would have had her mother wrapped around his little finger. Her mother passed at the young age of forty-nine due to breast cancer.

Deja thought she had been devastated when her mother died, and then her father, Stoney Scarlett, passed away a year later from what Deja was sure was a broken heart. Deja was left to make her way through this world on her own. Her father just wasn't the same after the passing of his wife. She had been nineteen years old when her father took his last breath.

"I'll call you back and let you know," Deja chuckled, wiping the lone tear that blazed a trail down her cheek. "I just feel bad if you were to have to keep him—"

"Now you know, little August is a treat to have. It's no problem. I'd rather have you safely tucked away in the hotel than crashed in some ditch, freezing to death. I have plenty of milk and diapers to get him through the night, and I have my other grandkids tonight to give my daughter and her husband a break. He's fine."

"Okay, Sharon. I'll call you a little later. I'm going to see if they'll even let me off early, and if not, get a room if it gets too bad." Deja disconnected the call after they said their goodbyes and pushed off the wall. She knew there was a slim chance that she'd be able to get off early.

She walked back out, into the main part of the restaurant. Ski Bar and Grille was a large bar that patrons could have a good time in on the mountain. With a bar, pool table, and good food, it usually stayed packed. It was decorated like a large hunting lodge, with a roaring fire in one of the large fireplaces that lined the wall to help fight off the cold.

"Hey, Deja. You have a couple of guys who asked to be seated in your area," Alana said with a wink.

"Really?" Deja readjusted her apron in front of

her as she walked toward the bar. "Why my section? The whole restaurant is open for them to sit anywhere."

"I don't know, but they're two tall, dark, and handsome men. If you're refusing them, I will gladly—"

Deja glanced at the table and froze in disbelief.

"I'll take it," she murmured as she stared at the two figures seated at the table.

It couldn't be.

She silently cursed herself for throwing her hair up in a messy bun today before work. She sent up a prayer of thanks that she had actually had a few minutes to shower. She blew out a deep breath and headed in the direction of the person whose eyes she got to look into every single day.

Augie's father had returned.

The tall, muscular figure turned around and his amber eyes hit hers, taking her breath away.

Dixon.

Dixon's tiger let loose a growl as his eyes greedily took in Deja as she made her way to him. Her body was curvier than he remembered. His slow perusal of her had his cock growing stiff with need. Her breasts had become fuller. He remembered how they fit in his large hands perfectly. His eyes continued their descent down her body and found her hips to be rounder. He liked the new look of her body.

He loved for his women to have curves, and Deja had them in all the right places. His only complaint was the dark circles beneath her eyes. His tiger stood at attention, not liking the fact that she hadn't been getting restful sleep.

"Well hello," she breathed as she stood at the table, a faint smile ghosting her lips.

He froze in place and didn't know what to say. It was as if his brain had left him. Only his cock stood at attention, and he knew he couldn't lead with that. He just stared at her, trying to take her in.

"Well, apparently, the cat has my good friend's tongue. I'm Percy," Percy chuckled, reaching his hand out to Deja.

A genuine smile crossed her face as she laughed. She reached out and took Percy's hand in a handshake.

"I remember you guys. You were here last year around this same time. What brings you back two years in a row?" she asked. She turned to him, and he could have sworn something passed through her eyes, but he couldn't put a finger on what it meant exactly.

"An annual meeting," he blurted out, finally able to speak. Her eyes widened slightly.

"In this weather? I haven't heard of any conventions around Christmastime around here," she noted. He held back a groan as she pulled her bottom lip between her teeth. He ached to be the one to take his tongue and soothe her plump lips.

"It's an unofficial meeting of sorts." He couldn't tear his eyes off of her. She was just as beautiful as he remembered. His fingers itched to remove her hair from the large bun on top of her head. His tiger clawed at his chest, begging to get out so that he could go to her.

He breathed in her scent, and it relaxed his animal, but only a little. It was the same scent that he knew was hers, but it was slightly different. He couldn't put his finger on it, so he shook it off. It had been a year since he saw her, so maybe his memory was slightly off.

"How long are you going to be here, Dixon?" she asked softly, holding her small notebook against her chest.

As long as it takes to convince you to come with me, he thought to himself. He instead basked in the glow of hearing her say his name.

She did remember, he thought.

"A few days," he said. Tomorrow, he and the council would meet for their annual retreat, then afterwards, he would start his wooing of her to win her over.

Even though tigers were known to be solitary animals in the wild, their shifter counterparts were a little more social. Dixon was considered royalty among the shifter worlds. His family had been head of the council for centuries.

The council consisted of prominent members of the tiger shifter community around the country. Each year, they got together to discuss issues in the community. The meeting was also a way for them to fraternize with each other, to reinforce the trust between members. The seven members would meet tomorrow at the main lodge.

"Well, what can I get you fellas?" she asked.

You.

He held his tongue and glanced down at the menu quickly, while Percy gave her his order. She turned to him and he ordered his food. He wasn't truly hungry, but he knew that he needed to feed his animal. Tonight, he'd do whatever he must to have her leave with him.

"I'll be back soon with your drinks." She smiled before walking off. His eyes narrowed in on her round ass as she walked away.

His animal rumbled low in his chest.

She would be his.

CHAPTER THREE

"Girl, you've been holding out. You know those two delicious hunks?" Alana sighed as she leaned against the bar. She wasn't even hiding the fact that she was ogling the two.

Deja wiped the counter down, needing to keep busy. Since they weren't busy, she opted to help Luna with cleaning the bar so that it would be done by the time they could leave. Luna had left a message with their manager, and they were waiting to see if they would close early.

"Sort of," Deja murmured. She wasn't too far from the truth. She may not *know* him, but from the little time they did have together, she had memorized every muscular ridge of his abdomen, what made him groan, and what made his body tremble during the heat of passion. She looked up and found his eyes on her. A small smile played on her lips as she returned his gaze.

She knew this was her chance.

She had to tell him about Augie.

Dread filled her stomach at the thought. Would he accept their son? Does he already have a family? She didn't see a ring on his finger, but knew that really didn't mean anything.

It didn't matter. He deserved to know about the son he had helped create. If he chose to walk away, it would hurt, but she would keep on raising her son alone as she had planned to do.

"How? I certainly haven't seen them around before." Deja could feel her co-worker's eyes on her. "I would have remembered them."

"They came in here a year ago with some friends. That's it." Deja pushed her hair behind her ear as she tossed the dishcloth in the sink.

She didn't want to go into too much detail about how she knew them. She didn't want the girls to get suspicious and start calculating Augie's conception and birth. None of her friends knew who August's father was. She had kept it a secret. She didn't want to admit that August was a mistake. He was her little gift that Dixon had left her. She had always been an optimistic person and saw August as a chance to have a family. He was her focus.

The girls had been trying to get Deja to go out on dates, but it was a little hard to date a woman who was pregnant by another man. Ever since August was born, Luna, Alana, and Niki had been trying to throw her back into the dating pool.

"Boss said after these two, we can close up. Roads are closing," Luna announced as she came from the back office.

"What?" Deja gasped. She walked over to glance out the window near the parking lot and could barely see through the flurries. Her car was literally buried beneath a few feet of snow.

There was no way that she would be able to get off the mountain tonight.

She groaned and pulled her cell phone out. She sent out a quick text to Sharon that she would be grabbing a room at the hotel. She hated the thought of Augie being without her for a night, but she knew Sharon was right. It was better for only one night to be away from him than a whole lifetime of absence from a mother because she was foolish enough to try to fight through snow on a dark mountain road.

Her phone pinged a return message, and it was Sharon, wishing her good night. She sighed and brushed her hair from her face as she turned back to Dixon's table.

Her heart slammed against her chest as she strolled over to him and his friend. She rubbed her sweaty hands on her apron as she approached their table.

"How's everything?" she asked nervously. She glanced at Dixon, and his intense eyes took her breath away. She had never seen such an eye color before. Augie's eyes were the exact same as his, and she knew that she had to tell him.

Tonight.

She may never get the chance again, and didn't want to miss out on it.

"We're good. Almost done," Percy announced with a smile.

"How have you been, Deja?" Dixon asked, his eyes filled with concern. "You look tired."

"I've been doing okay. Just working a lot. Trying to make ends meet." She smiled.

Working and taking care of our child, she wanted to say, but held back. That wasn't how she wanted to tell him. Her mind raced, trying to figure out how she would tell him that he was a father.

"Have a seat with us." He waved his hand to the

seat next to him. "Doesn't look like there are any other customers. Rest your feet."

She glanced over at the bar to find that Alana had disappeared. It wouldn't hurt her sitting down to speak with them. There was no one else in the bar. She was sure the girls were in the back helping break down the kitchen with the cook, Axel.

"Sure." She took the seat next to him and had to hold back a sigh as she took in the scent of him. It was just as she remembered. Dixon was all man. "Where are you staying while you're here? The roads are nasty out there."

Make small talk with them. She figured she'd find out which lodge he was staying in and meet him there sometime tomorrow.

Dixon placed his fork down, finished with his meal. He leaned back against the booth and placed his arm along the back, putting her in the crook of his arm. She held back a groan, feeling the heat from his body. She ached to lean into him and nuzzle her face against his. She just wanted to smell him. She glanced up at him and saw his eyes darken, as if he knew what she was thinking.

Her body was reacting to his. Her breasts tingled as her nipples grew into hard little buds, pushing against her bra. She could feel moisture collecting at the apex of her thighs. One look was all it took, just as it did a year ago. She swallowed hard as she met his gaze.

She wanted him.

But she couldn't.

The product of their desire was currently spending the night at the babysitter's house.

"We're staying at the Rocky Lodge," Dixon murmured. A shiver passed through her as his fingers connected with a few strands of her hair. He was staying at the same hotel as last year where they created Augie. Her breath caught in her throat as memories of that night came to mind.

"It looks bad out. Do you have far to go to get home?" Percy asked. Deja finally tore her eyes away from Dixon. Her breaths were coming fast. She was fairly certain he was thinking of their night together as well, and looking into his eyes, she knew he was wanting a repeat.

She couldn't.

"Um, I live at the bottom of the mountain. Luna just said that the roads on the mountain are closed, so I'm going to have to get a room. Thank goodness we get free rooms when the snow gets too bad in the winter here. I certainly couldn't afford to stay here." She gave a nervous chuckle.

"That's nice of them." Percy nodded, finishing off his drink. "Are you from here?"

"No, Denver. I moved here to be closer to my job instead of driving almost an hour every day for work. You guys are from Cleveland, right?" she asked with a nervous laugh. "I've never been, but I'm told winters there can be just as bad as here."

"They can be." Percy nodded and laughed.

"When are you getting off?" Dixon asked, drawing her attention back to him.

"According to Luna, as soon as you two are done, we get to close up and leave."

"Well, I'm certainly done. That food was fabulous. Please give my compliments to the chef." Percy stood from the table and pulled his wallet out. He tossed a few bills onto the table. "I got dinner tonight, my friend."

"I'll see you in the morning." Dixon nodded to his friend as he left, leaving the two of them alone. She smiled and waved to Percy as he made his way through the restaurant.

She turned back to Dixon, unsure of what to do next.

"I've thought of you this past year," he murmured, his fingers still playing with her hair. She ached to pull it down so that he could thread his fingers through it. She tried to steer her thoughts away from all the sexy carnal thoughts that were running through her mind, but she was losing the battle.

"Really? You've been on my mind too," she admitted. She shifted so that she could face him, knowing that she needed to pull up her big girl panties and tell him. "Can we go somewhere to talk?"

His eyes darkened, and she knew what he was thinking. She was trying to keep this neutral and find a quiet place so that they could talk.

"Want to go back to my room?" he asked.

She swallowed hard. That wasn't the best idea, but it would give them some privacy for the talk they needed to have. She would behave herself and not jump his bones the minute they were alone. She was an adult, as was he. They could be in a hotel room and not have sex.

That was her mind talking.

Her heart, on the other hand, was screaming for her to strip him naked and have her way with him.

"Sure."

CHAPTER FOUR

Dixon waited for Deja to finish closing up. The hotel he was staying in was a quick walk from the bar and grille. Earlier that day he had stopped in, but she hadn't come on shift yet. He and Percy had spent the day skiing since they had arrived a day earlier than the rest of the council members.

He barely felt the cold as he watched Deja come out of the restaurant. The snow had stopped falling at the moment. Since that morning, the sky had dumped at least another two feet. His eyes were locked on Deja as she spoke to her friends.

His tiger snarled as she hugged the guy who must have been the cook. He didn't like the way the guy whispered into her ear. He wanted to run over there and tear the guy apart. He bit back a growl as she began to make her way toward him. He could see that her friends were curious, but they turned and walked down the opposite path.

"Hey," she said shyly. She pulled her coat tighter as the wind blew past them.

"Where's your hat?" he asked, feeling his protectiveness for her coming to the forefront. Unable to keep from touching her, he grabbed her hand and pulled her close to him. He knew that as a shifter, his body ran warmer than a human. She buried herself in his side as they began the walk to his hotel.

His chest rumbled from his tiger, loving the feel of her pressed up against him. They fit perfectly together. She was so tiny compared to his almost six and a half foot frame.

"I don't have one. I lost it a week ago and just haven't gotten around to buying a new one yet." She laughed. He tried to use his body to shield her from the cold as they picked up speed. "How are you so warm? You're like a furnace!"

"I don't know," he lied, pulling her closer. His cock was rock hard, just thinking of peeling her out of her clothes. He wanted to see if her body was as he had imagined it being all this time.

Minutes later, they were walking through the lobby of the hotel. He led her to the elevator and hit the button, then ushered her inside. He refused to let her hand go. Anticipation for what was to come had his heart racing.

He had tried to live his life after her, but no other woman compared to Deja. Now that he finally had her back in his grasp, he refused to leave Breckenridge without her. They arrived on his floor and he pulled her behind him, then pulled his keycard from his jacket as they arrived at his suite. He opened the door and waved her in.

His heart had slammed against his chest when she'd asked for them to talk. They would have plenty of time to talk tonight, but right now, he needed her naked and spread out on his bed for him to feast on her curvy body.

"These suites always amaze me," she breathed as she walked in. He closed the door behind them and flipped on the light. The suite was plush, consisting of a living room, dining area, private bedroom, and two bathrooms. The balcony even had a hot tub that he had fantasied about them using.

He shrugged off his jacket and tossed it on the back of one of the dining chairs before moving to her to help her remove her jacket.

"What did you want to talk about?" he murmured, trying to calm his beast. He took her jacket and placed it on the back of another chair. He watched her walk around the living area before making her way to the patio doors. She paused in front of the large glass doors that displayed the mountains. The snow had begun to fall again.

"We had one night last year together, and I don't even know your last name," she said softly. He watched as she reached out a hand to place it on the glass, as if trying to touch the snow.

"Blackburn," he answered, moving toward her. "What's yours?"

"Scarlett."

She reached up and pulled her hair from the bun. He held back a groan as he watched her dark hair cascade around her shoulders. He loved her hair. It was thick, soft, and silky. He wanted to feel it brush against his naked skin as it did before. He could remember her blazing a hot trail of kisses down his chest as she went further, before taking him deep into her mouth.

His jeans grew tight, his cock demanding to be set free as he stood next to her.

"It's nice to meet you, Deja Scarlett," he murmured, holding his hand out to her.

"Likewise, Dixon Blackburn." She smiled, taking his hand. The jolt of electricity that ran up his arm from their touch caused his tiger to pace. It knew their mate was in front of them. It wanted to claim her now. But they couldn't. Humans didn't know of shifters or the paranormal world. If she accepted him, then he would have to tell her.

"I thought about contacting you, but wasn't sure it would be welcomed," she said, glancing away from him as she let his hand go. He could see a red tint appear on her cheeks.

"Why would you think that?" he asked. He reached out and turned her back to face him.

"I figured someone like you wouldn't want anything to do with me, that I was just a passing fancy while you were on vacation with your friends. We didn't exchange last names or numbers. There was no promise of anything, which I was okay with. Not that I'm complaining. I knew what I was getting into last year," she said.

His tiger slammed into his chest.

She had wanted to contact him.

He reached up a hand and brushed her hair from her face, feeling regret fill his chest for the thousandth time. He should have made sure she had his contact information.

"What do you mean, someone like me?" He frowned down at her as she stepped closer to him.

"I'm just a small-town waitress and you are you. I

don't know what you do for a living, but it seems to me that you're someone important. Besides what we shared, what would you want with me?"

Forever, a voice screamed in the back of his mind.

He stepped closer to her. Cupping her face with his hands, he lowered his head to hers, covering her mouth with his. Her lips were as soft as he remembered. She gasped, opening her lips for him to allow his tongue to enter her mouth. He swept the inside, learning her taste all over again.

He had dreamt of this night for months. He was given a second chance, and this time, he was not letting Deja slip through his fingers again.

He held her face tight in his grasp as he tilted his head to deepen the kiss. They were quickly spiraling out of control. He knew she had wanted to talk, but right now, he needed her. His fingers slipped beneath her shirt. He pulled it up and over her head, breaking their kiss.

"Deja," he breathed, taking in the picture of her in jeans and lace bra. He saw the clasp nestled in between her breasts. He reached up and gently undid it, freeing her bountiful breasts, and pushed the restricting material to the floor.

He released a growl as he scooped her up in his

arms. He rushed into the bedroom and laid her on the bed before reaching for the lamp on the nightstand to flick it on. He wanted to see her.

"Dixon," she moaned as he removed her shoes and socks. "Hurry."

"I'm taking my time tonight," he growled, removing the rest of her clothes. The sight of her on the bed, naked, with her hair spread out against the white comforter was the exact image that he imagined in his mind.

"You have too many clothes on." She gave a husky chuckle as she looked at him.

He stripped his clothes off before reaching for her. His cock was stiff and ready. He could scent her arousal and knew that she was ready for him, but he just had to taste her first. He had been dying to have the taste of Deja Scarlett on his lips again.

Dixon pulled her to the edge of the bed and her legs fell apart, revealing her glistening pussy. His chest rumbled at the beautiful sight. He dipped his head down to feast on his woman.

CHAPTER FIVE

Deja's back arched off the bed with the first swipe of Dixon's wide tongue.

"Dixon," she moaned as he held her legs apart. Her plans had flown out the window the moment his lips had touched hers. She had waited for this moment for the past year. She needed this man, and here he was with his head buried in between her thighs.

She cried out as his tongue circled her sensitive bundle of nerves. She thrust her hips toward his face, trying to ensure he could reach every facet of her pussy with his magical tongue. She could feel the moisture seep out of her as he worked her over.

Her breaths came fast as he sucked on her clit and slid a finger deep within her. Her muscles clenched on his finger as he thrust it in and out of her, while his mouth focused on her clit.

"You taste just like I remember." His deep guttural growls turned her on even more. It was as if he had an animalistic side of him trying to come to the forefront. She remembered his growls of pleasure. Her core clenched with the thought. "So sweet. So wet. So...mine."

"Dixon...God!" she groaned as he introduced another finger. In the back of her mind, she knew he was trying to ensure that she was prepped for his wide girth. She began to tremble from the sensations that rocked her body. Her skin prickled with the familiar feel of her orgasm approaching.

"Has anyone else tasted this sweet pussy since me?"

"No," she gasped, throwing her head back in ecstasy. His growl signaled his pleasure as he continued his feast between her legs. Of course there was no one else. She'd been pregnant, then busy working, while trying to take care of a three-month-old. Most men would shy away from a woman like her.

"Say my name again," he growled against her pussy lips as she thrust her hips in rhythm, riding his face and hand.

"Dixon, please," she gasped as she shook. Her body arched again as he twisted his fingers around, hitting a certain spot in her core that sent her almost flying off the bed.

"Please what?"

She squeezed her eyes shut as she spread her legs as wide as she could. He latched onto her clit and refused to let up.

"Make me come!" she cried out as her orgasm rocked through her. She flew into euphoric heaven as her orgasm stole all the breath from her body.

There had been no one else after him, and every orgasm she had were compliments of her own fingers or vibrator, and always to the memory of their last encounter.

If this was the only time she would get to have him again, she would take what she could get. She gripped his hair in her hand as she rode out the waves of her orgasm.

She chanted his name as he pulled from her and crawled over her body, her legs falling apart to accommodate him.

His lips slammed onto hers in a brutal kiss as his cock slid home. She cried out from the feeling of being stretched by him. He paused, allowing her to get used to the slight burn of her pussy acclimating itself to his girth.

He growled low in her ear as he pulled back and slammed into her, hard.

"Dixon!" she cried out.

"Deja," he moaned as his hips began to move fast and hard.

This was a year of sexual need built up for this man, and she couldn't get enough of him. Her hips met his thrust for thrust as she wrapped her legs around him.

"Yes," she groaned as he tore his lips from hers to trail hot kisses alongside her jaw and to the crook of her neck. She buried her fingers in his hair, trying to hold on for the ride as their bodies rocked together in the age-old dance.

Tonight, Dixon Blackburn was truly fucking her.

This wasn't sweet love they were making. No, he was consuming her. Dixon was leaving his mark on her. No other's would compare.

He rolled them on the bed, putting her on top of him. He was still buried deep within her.

"Ride me, Deja," he ordered, his intense eyes locked on hers. His hands gripped her hips to help guide her. The new position allowed his cock to go even deeper.

"Yes," she gasped, leaning forward to brace her hands over his head as she lifted her hips up. He guided her down on him as he thrust up inside of her. The feel of his thick cock slipping inside of her from this angle had her gasping for breath. She could feel the waves of her orgasm returning.

He quickened his pace, thrusting his cock deeper. He caught her nipple in his mouth and sucked. A shudder passed through her body as he sucked on her aching breast.

"Oh my God. I'm going to come again." Her body shook as her orgasm took over. She screamed as her core pulsated from the sensations of his length stretching her pussy walls.

He roared through his release, shooting his seed deep within her. He thrust a few more times as he filled her.

Her breaths came fast as she laid on his hard chest. She closed her eyes, knowing that this had been a beautiful mistake.

She'd lost track of time as they lied together, his semisoft length still buried deep inside of her. She didn't want to move to dislodge him from her. They fit perfectly together.

His hand reached up and brushed her hair from her face.

"Are you okay?" he murmured. She opened her eyes and met his. She nodded, unable to speak. She was afraid that if she opened her mouth, she would blurt out everything, and now was not the time to tell him that they had created a child together. "Stay with me tonight."

She leaned back to look into the amber eyes that were identical to their son's. Just like Augie, she could never refuse this man anything. She nodded her head.

A grin spread across his face as he flipped them over, somehow leaving them connected. She could feel him growing hard within her as he braced himself over her.

"Again?" she gasped in disbelief as he gripped her wrists and brought them over her head, causing her breasts to thrust out.

"Yes," he growled, taking one of her mounds into his mouth. "Again and again, until neither of us can walk in the morning. And even then, one more time."

Deja opened her eyes and cringed as the daylight flooded the room. She stared up at the ceiling, unable to believe that she had slept with Dixon again. She could see if, maybe, she had the excuse of being tipsy or drunk, but she hadn't had a sip of alcohol since before she got pregnant.

Nope, it was all her fault.

She glanced over at the sleeping Dixon and felt a sharp stabbing pain in her chest. She knew he had some important meeting today. They didn't do much talking last night. The sex between the two of them had been desperate, hard, and definitely fulfilling.

Deja could feel the soreness between her thighs. Dixon was a man who knew how to ensure a woman was pleased by the time she left his bed. She glanced over at the clock and felt her heart stop.

It was almost ten a.m., so she scrambled from the bed as quietly as she could and grabbed her clothes. She hopped into her jeans as quietly as she could. She didn't know where her panties were, and didn't have time to look for them. She was sure Sharon would be worried sick about her. She jogged around the suite and found her bra and shirt. She made her way back to the bedroom to hear the slight sounds of Dixon's snores filling the air.

She bit her lip. She didn't want to wake him. She didn't want to explain at the moment that she had to rush off to the babysitter's. Her eyes blurred with tears as she leaned her head against the doorjamb, unsure of what to do.

Should she tell him about Augie?

He said that he would be in town for a few more days. If he was truly interested in her, he knew where she worked. She turned and grabbed her coat and purse and walked out of his suite.

CHAPTER SIX

Dixon snarled as he slowly made his way down the mountain in his rented SUV. He woke up, content from having spent the night with Deja. To wake up and find her gone put him in a bad mood.

Not this time.

His tiger paced, wanting her back at their side. She should have known that he didn't want this to be another one-night stand. The intensity of their lovemaking should have been a clue. It was something that one didn't throw away, but held on to tight.

Not having a clue of where she lived, he had to look her up. At least now he knew her last name. He found her address in the directory. It took him a good while to slowly make his way down the mountain. He had called Percy and had him push the meeting back to later this afternoon for an early dinner meeting.

He had to go after his mate.

He finally reached the base of the mountain and followed the GPS directions to her house. He found her house easy enough, but didn't see a car in her driveway. He parked a few houses down and waited. He was sure that she didn't have to work this early. It was almost noon.

What if she did have to work and raced off to her job so that she wouldn't get in trouble?

He glanced around her neighborhood, truly seeing it for the first time. It wasn't much. It wasn't rundown, and the neighbors seemed to have pride in their small homes and yards. Most yards were decorated with Christmas decorations in celebration of the upcoming holiday.

He would take her from this and give her whatever she wanted in the world. His home in Cleveland was massive, but felt empty with just him in it. He would convince Deja to mate with him.

They would have to have that talk she had wanted. There was so much he would have to explain to her about shifters and mating. He ached to put his mark on her. A scratch or bite would mark her as his forever.

His tiger paced beneath his skin. He would need to shift soon. His beast was getting anxious to break free, and the call of the snow and woods was making it harder not to shift.

The sound of his phone ringing filled the air. He glanced down at it and saw Percy calling.

"Yeah?"

"We got a problem," Percy announced. The hairs on the back of his neck rose at the announcement.

"What is it?"

"I'm not sure why, but lion shifters have been spotted in the area."

There had been a long-standing feud between tiger and lion shifters. The two powerful feline groups did not get along. Currently, the tigers held one of the top seats on the Paranormal League Committee. The PLC was an organization that had all shifters represented, and Dixon currently sat on it, representing the feline shifters.

"You have to be shitting me," he growled. Movement along the road grabbed his attention. A small sedan made it's way down the snow-covered road. "What the hell would Tyson's men be here for?"

Tyson Rollins, alpha of the lion pride, made it his life's work to try to discredit Dixon. The lion shifter wanted to have Dixon's seat on the PLC and didn't care how he got it. Dixon wouldn't be surprised if the lion shifter had someone tailing him to catch him in some act that he could turn around and use against Dixon to win the seat.

"I'm not sure, but I'll find out. There's no reason why lions should be here in Breckenridge. I didn't even think they liked the snow," Percy replied.

"Find out why they're here." His eyes followed the sedan as it pulled into Deja's driveway. His heart pounded in his chest as he watched Deja step from the driver's seat and make her way around to the back passenger door. He disconnected the call and turned the truck off.

"She went grocery shopping," he muttered to himself. He moved to leave the warmth of the vehicle when his heart lodged in his throat.

She pulled a baby carrier from the back seat and tossed a baby bag over her shoulder. He sat frozen as he watched her scurry to the house. It took her a few seconds before she was able to gain entrance into the tiny home.

"She has a job as a babysitter too?" The words didn't sit right on his tongue, but her comments about not affording certain things last night came to mind. His anger at her leaving this morning dissipated at the thought that she had left for work.

She could have at least left a note or something. He chuckled at his thoughts. Percy would have his balls if he knew the thoughts that were flowing through his mind.

Well, if she had to have two jobs to make ends meet, then so be it.

He stepped out the vehicle and made his way to her house.

His mate, once she accepted him, would never have to work again if she didn't want to. He could provide any and everything she could possibly want. The Blackburn family was from old money. Their wealth spanned generations of Blackburn's, and he would continue that legacy with the family business.

"She would have to accept us," his tiger growled in his head.

"I know," he muttered, reaching the door. He rang the doorbell, ready to confront his little disappearing artist.

"Hey, Momma's little man," Deja cooed as she took Augie from his carrier. His amber eyes met hers, and a smile flashed across his face. "Was that a smile, or do you have gas?"

Her heart was so filled with love for this little man, that she was surprised she didn't burst. The minute she even thought of her son, a smile would spread across her face.

"Guess what, Augie? Mommy saw your daddy last night. You are the spitting image of him." She nuzzled his soft hair with her cheek. She knew her son didn't understand a word she was saying, but it didn't keep her from talking out loud to him. She had read that talking to babies early on helped with their language development.

Being away from him so long just made her want to cuddle with him on the couch for a little while. He began to fuss, and she knew it was time to feed him.

Her breasts ached from not being able to pump since last night at work on her break. She had sent up a prayer when she was with Dixon that she wouldn't leak out on him. That would have been awkward, and would have certainly needed an explanation. She had to be careful about that. She didn't want her milk to dry up. She wanted to go as long as she could to breastfeed Augie. She lived for the private, intimate moments she got to have with him as she fed him.

He began to root around on her chest as she moved to the couch.

The door bell chimed.

"Well, who could that be?" she murmured, holding Augie close to her as she headed toward the door.

Before picking him up from Sharon's, she had stopped home to take a five-minute shower and change her clothes. She didn't want to show up to Sharon's looking like she had been royally fucked all night.

She patted her damp hair as she reached for the door handle. She opened the door and froze in place.

Dixon.

"Deja," he murmured, his eyes locked on the back of Augie's head.

"Dixon. How did you know where I lived?" she asked quietly. Her heart raced as she stared at him.

"I was able to look up your address," he replied, his eyes not moving from August's head.

This was the moment.

She had no way to get out of this.

"I think you need to come in so that we can have that talk," she whispered, unlocking the security screen door. She pushed it open and moved back so that he could enter her home. She looked around, knowing that she didn't have much, but she kept her house clean and tidy. She would describe it as cozy. It was just big enough for her and a baby. Eventually, she would have to find them somewhere else to live once August got bigger and unable to sleep in a crib.

Fear filled her at his reaction. A pained expression was on his face. Panic began to rise in her chest.

"Please, have a seat," she offered as she locked the door and moved to the couch, leaving the loveseat for him to have. She took her seat, just as Augie chose that moment to fuss, wanting his food.

"He's mine," Dixon stated, his eyes finally moving to hers.

She was taken aback. How would he know that right away? She closed her eyes as August began to cry.

It was time.

"Yes," she whispered as tears filled her eyes. She glanced down at Augie's red face as his crying grew louder.

She had dreamt of this moment so many times and how it would go, but crying was not in any of them.

"Can I?" he asked, holding his hands out to her. His eyes were filled with pain. She hesitated for a moment at his outstretched hands. She placed a kiss on her son's head, as the tears began to fall and blaze hot trails down her cheeks.

She stood so that she could transfer Augie to his father, and quietly watched as Dixon carefully cradled their child to his chest. She bit back a sob as he gazed down at August.

Amazed, she watched as August's cries began to lessen as their eyes met.

Father and son were meeting for the first time.

She brushed the tears from her eyes, not wanting to spoil the moment for Dixon.

August stared up at his father. Their expressions were similar as they sized each other up.

"How old is he?" Dixon asked, his voice low. He had yet to look back at her.

"Three months."

"What is his name?" Dixon leaned down and placed his forehead against Augie's.

"August Dixon Scarlett," she whispered, her voice ending on a squeak at the picture they made.

Father and son, bonding.

Dixon pulled back and looked over at her.

"My middle name is August," he admitted.

A gasp escaped her at the announcement. There was no way she would have known that.

She expected to see hatred in his eyes, or disgust, but no. This was a quiet, reserved Dixon.

He must be in shock, she thought.

She watched, guarded, as he walked to her. He cradled August, who seemed to settle against his chest. Dixon reached for her and pulled her against his chest. This was what her and August were missing.

"I'm so sorry, Deja," he murmured against her head.

A sob tore from her soul as the waterworks flowed. Her body was racked with sobs as she leaned into Dixon. She wasn't sure what the future would hold, but she would take this moment of being held by him, along with their child, as if they were a family.

This moment would be forever burned into her memory.

CHAPTER SEVEN

Dixon sat frozen in Deja's living room as she went to lay August down in his crib. Dixon leaned forward with his head braced in his hands.

A son.

He had a son.

The minute Deja had opened the door and August's scent hit him, he knew that he was his child. A shifter never needed a paternity test. Their offspring would always carry their parent's scent.

His heart ached that he had missed so much. It was his fault. Realization hit him square in his chest. His animal knew that they had impregnated Deja. That was why a few months ago, his tiger began to pace and become almost uncontrollable.

His son had entered into the world.

His son.

If only he had given Deja his contact number

before leaving a year ago, all of this would have progressed differently. Dixon's heart was heavy, thinking that Deja had to do it all by herself. Who was there when she found out she was pregnant? Was she happy about it? Was she sad? Did she have a rough pregnancy? Was she by herself when she gave birth?

So many thoughts raced through his head as he waited for her to come out the room. She had allowed him to watch her feed August. It was one of the greatest moments of his life, watching his son receiving his nourishment from Deja's breasts. He was fascinated at how his son became drunk on his mother's milk and dozed off to sleep.

Yes, they needed to talk.

Had he never returned to Breckenridge, his son would have grown up fatherless.

Unless Deja would have married someone else, then his son would have been raised by another man.

His animal released a deep growl at the thought of another man around his son.

He had to tell her about his animal. Just one look at August and he knew his genes were strong. August was half-shifter, and would have the ability to shift when he got older.

"He's still asleep," Deja announced as she

walked back into the small living area. She sat down on the small plush chair and tucked her feet underneath her.

He nodded, but finally looked at her, as if seeing her for the first time. Those dark areas beneath her eyes weren't that of working too much. They were from the strain of being a single mother and working to make ends meet to provide for her and August.

No more.

What was his, was hers. She was his mate, and she had given him the greatest gift anyone could have ever given him. Christmas was a few days away, and little August was his gift.

"We need to talk about August…" he began. He could see the apprehension in her eyes as she nodded. He needed to ease her mind first. "First, I would never try to take him from you, but I would like to be a part of his life."

"Of course." Relief flooded her face. "Whatever you want to do. I'm just happy that you want to be a part of his life. I've dreamt of the moment when I would be able to get a hold of you and tell you. I was afraid that you were married —"

She gasped and her eyes flew to him.

"No, never married, and no kids," he assured her. He could understand why she would have to ask. A one-night stand while he was away on vacation did seem suspicious.

"Well, I'm glad that you want to be a part of his life," she continued. "Do you want to do a paternity test or something? I mean, I don't want you thinking that I'm taking advantage of you."

He ached to go to her, but he knew he needed to keep his hands off her so that they could finish their discussion.

"He's the spitting image of me. He even has my eyes," he said to her. "Plus, I need to tell you something about him. Something about me."

Her eyes widened as she waited for him to go on. He knew he was about to tell her something that she wouldn't believe.

"What could you tell me about Augie that I don't already know?"

"My genes are the strongest between the two of us..." he began.

"Tell me something I don't already know," she muttered, looking down at her hands. "If I wouldn't have seen him come out of me, I would question who carried him."

He was pleased that she was getting to the point of joking because what he was about to tell her was going to blow her mind.

"My family...we carry certain genes that will make August different as he gets older."

"What?" She sat forward in the chair, her eyes panicked.

"It's nothing to worry about. He'll be fine. What he is, I am too." He tried to keep his voice low and soothing, not wanting her to panic, but it was too late.

"What does that mean? My son is a little boy. You're a man. He'll grow into a man. We all know that."

Dixon closed his eyes briefly. Opening them, he met her confused ones.

"Even though August doesn't have my last name, he is a Blackburn. He's my heir, and my genes will always dominate a human's. My son is a shifter. A tiger shifter. As am I."

CHAPTER EIGHT

Deja blinked her eyes as she stared at Dixon.
What did he just say?

There was no way that she heard him say what she thought he said. A shifter? A tiger shifter? She stared at Dixon in shock at first, but then she smiled.

A nervous laugh escaped her as she stared at the man that helped her create her perfect little bundle of joy, who was resting quietly in the other room. She must be losing her mind.

"You're joking, right?" She smiled at him, waiting for him to crack a joke or something, but he stared at her with a serious look. Her smile slowly faded as she waited. She jumped as he stood, and began to move her furniture out the way. He pushed her fake Christmas tree far back into the corner of the room. "What are you doing?"

Once he was satisfied, he began to strip his clothes off. She was baffled at his behavior.

"Dixon—"

"Please, Deja. Just sit. I'll explain everything in a few minutes."

She plopped down as he tossed his clothes onto her small loveseat. Once he was fully naked in front of her, she tried to keep her eyes from dropping to take a quick peek at his cock, but failed. She squeezed her thighs together at the sight of his thick length hanging in between his legs.

"Eyes up here," he announced. Her eyes flew to his. "Don't be afraid. He won't hurt you."

Her face grew warm as her eyes met his. She saw the twinkle in his eyes before the air seemed to shimmer around him. Her eyes widened at the sound of bones rearranging. Orange fur burst forward on his skin. She gasped as Dixon fell to the floor, and within seconds, a massive tiger stood in front of her.

"Oh my God," she whispered, frozen in place. Her eyes met that of the tiger's, and she saw Dixon in them. "Dixon?"

Her heart thumped against her chest as the tiger came toward her. She scooted back in the chair, afraid of being eaten by the massive cat.

He growled low in his throat as he stopped in front of the chair.

"Don't be afraid" Dixon had said.

The tiger paused and tilted his head, as if to ask her to scratch his head. She reached out a hesitant hand and ran her fingers through his thick fur. She laughed as his chest rumbled. She scratched behind his ear, and he turned his head to lick her hand with his long tongue.

She blew out a deep breath as she met the tiger's eyes. She could see Dixon in them. They were the same amber as his and Augie's.

Her son would be like his father.

Her son would grow up to be a shifter.

Who knew that shifters truly existed?

The tiger turned as best he could in her small living room and headed off to the back room.

She scrambled from her chair and ran behind it, no longer afraid. She watched as he gently pushed the door to her bedroom open and crept into the room. She paused at the door and watched as the tiger stood next to the bed and breathed in her son's smell. He turned his massive head to her, and she would have sworn she'd seen pride in the tiger's eyes.

The air around the animal began to shimmer,

and she watched as the body reshaped itself and the fur disappeared, leaving Dixon kneeling on the floor.

"How?" she asked as he stood from the floor. He glanced back at Augie before motioning her back out of the room. She paused in the hallway as he closed the door, then he stepped up to her, pushing her against the wall.

She swallowed hard as she watched his head come toward hers, and his lips met hers in a gentle kiss. She sighed and leaned against him, meeting him for a hot, open-mouthed kiss. His tongue dueled with hers as it swept into her mouth. A deep moan erupted from her at the feel of his stiff member pressing against her stomach.

"I want you," he murmured against her lips. She opened her eyes and met his stare. She could barely think after that kiss. "I came back for you. To find you. To see what this was between us."

"It took you a long time." She smiled as she looked into his eyes. She saw the sincerity. Her heart pounded at his admission. He came back to find her? "But you have to answer me. How are you able to change into a massive animal?"

He cupped her cheeks as he stared down at her.

"I was born this way." He placed another kiss on her lips and led her back to the living room. He guided her to the loveseat before grabbing his jeans and slipping them on. She made a mental note that he didn't wear underwear.

He threw his shirt back on and sat next to her on the small couch. He pulled her over to him and placed her across his lap.

"How are you born this way? I mean, are there others like you?"

"There is much you need to know. First thing you need to know is that humans don't know about the paranormal world."

Dixon blew out a deep breath as he stood from the couch. Deja had left to go check on August, or Augie, as she sometimes called him. He grabbed his phone from his jacket and dialed Percy's number.

"Where the hell are you?" His friend's voice asked when he picked up. "The meeting started five minutes ago—"

"We got a problem," he interrupted.

His friend must have heard the urgency in his voice.

"What's going on?"

"The lions prowling around. I'm not sure how they know, but I think I know why they're here." Dixon walked over to the window near Deja's small fake tree and looked out. His keen shifter eyes took in the neighborhood in the darkening light. His tiger was pacing, and he didn't know why. His gut told him that something was off about the neighborhood.

"What's going on? What did you find out?" Percy asked, shushing the voices near him.

"I have a son," he admitted. Silence greeted him. "Hello?"

"I'm here. What did you say? I think something is wrong with the connection. I could have sworn you said you have a son."

"I have a son. A baby. He's three months old. She named him August." He couldn't help the proud feeling that spread through his chest at the thought that his son—his seed—was in the other room.

"The waitress?"

"Yes." He smiled as he thought of August's chubby cheeks and amber eyes. "He's beautiful, Percy. He looks just like me."

"Congratulations, man. That's awesome. That's why you were drawn to find Deja."

"Thanks, but I think that's why the lions are prowling around here. I'm not sure if they know about Deja and August, but they could be in danger."

He glanced out the window and saw another SUV parked a little ways down from him. He could see a shadow in the front seat with his keen shifter vision.

"What do you want to do?" Percy asked, waiting on the word from Dixon.

"I want to get them to safety first. It may or may not be anything, but I don't trust Tyson."

"Send me your location, and Mason and I will make our way to you."

"Give me a second." Dixon disconnected the call and sent his location to his best friend.

"Why would August and I be in danger?" Deja's voice appeared from behind him. He turned to her and sighed. He didn't want to start this fragile relationship out on a lie.

"There are some men who don't like me because of my position in our hierarchy of shifters," he admitted. There was much he'd have to teach her. Even if they never mated, she was the mother of his child, and would be in danger.

"What does that have to do with me? I'm not a shifter. I'm just a human." She gripped August close to her chest. He closed his eyes briefly before opening them again to look at her. He moved to her, needing to be close to her and August.

"A man by the name of Tyson Rollins is the leader of the lion shifters. He's a dangerous man who I have had to fight against ever since we both came into power. He will do whatever he feels he needs to do to ruin me."

"August and I would be your weakness?" she asked. The smell of her fear permeated the air.

"No need to fear anything." He gathered her close, needing to have them in his arms. "I will protect you with my life, as will Percy, the council, and my family."

"Why would they protect me? They don't even know me. I understand August since he's your son, but I'm not anything to you."

He tipped her chin up so that he could look directly into her eyes. "You are my mate. My people would die for you."

"That seems a little extreme," she chuckled nervously. Her smile faded as she saw he was serious. "I don't want anyone dying for me."

"Hopefully, it will never come to that. I have my men coming now to make sure that your place is secure. Tyson's men have been spotted here in

Breckenridge, and I don't want them finding out about you or August."

He could feel her eyes on him as he stared down at August. He couldn't stop touching him. His hand reached out and rubbed his son's back as he cooed and sucked on the back of his fist. Dixon smiled as he watched, fascinated as his son's sucking noises grew louder.

"Can I?" he asked, his eyes moving to hers. She nodded and gently passed him over. His tiger huffed, detecting that the baby was in his arms. He knew that his tiger rising to the surface would settle little August down. He may not shift yet, but his tiger would be there, deep down, and would recognize Dixon's.

"If you think that this Tyson guy is a real problem, what do suggest we do?" she asked.

"It might be best for you to leave Breckenridge. If they saw you with me, they may become curious about you, and I don't want you on Tyson's radar."

She nodded and began to pace the room. He hated that his problems were going to follow her and August, but it was the way of shifters. They weren't too far off from their wild counterparts. The strongest were the ones to survive.

"I can leave. I've been thinking of moving out of Breckenridge. I have a tiny nest egg set aside."

His heart leapt in his chest at the mention of her leaving. It didn't sound as if she were thinking of leaving with him though. He glanced down at August and found his eyes on him. He smiled at his son, but it faded when he looked back to Deja.

"Move where?" he asked slowly.

"Colorado Springs, with my best friend, Niki. She's been trying to get me to move with her. She'll be able to help me with Augie."

He swallowed hard, and unconsciously rubbed the baby's back as he stared at her.

"I was thinking of you moving in with me."

CHAPTER NINE

Deja sat on the couch as she listened to Dixon speak to his friend, Percy. They had walked around her home and yard, trying to determine if the bad men had been around her house.

"There was a black SUV parked a few spaces down from mine. I know someone was in it, and I'm pretty sure it was one of Tyson's men," Dixon informed Percy, and a man she was introduced to named Mason.

She eyed Dixon with the two men. She could tell that Dixon was in charge by the way the other two looked to him, as if he were the alpha. She snorted at the thought. Did they even have alpha or kings in the paranormal world? Dixon had spoken of power and a certain seat he held. She always knew that he was a person of importance, but seeing him with his men confirmed that he held a powerful position.

She didn't know if she could take any more shocking news. To find out that her son's father was a tiger shifter, and her son, was enough. But then to find out that there was an entire paranormal world out there and a war amongst shifters that would drag her and her child in the middle of took the cake.

At least she thought it would.

Then Dixon's bombshell of her moving in with him had her in information overload. She looked down at Augie's sleeping form and her heart softened.

Would it be best for him if they moved in with his father? Was this mating thing real? She knew there was a crazy pull between her and Dixon, but could she believe that it was fate? Right now, her life sounded like one of those crazy romance books. Hell, Dixon being a tiger shifter sounded as if it should be in a book. If she wouldn't have watched his transformation with her own eyes, she would have thought he was a little touched in the head at the notion of being a shapeshifter.

She gently brushed Augie's hair from his tiny forehead and sighed. She had feelings for Dixon, but she wasn't sure they were the deep, intense forever love that was mentioned in romance books. She glanced over at him and could see a future with him.

Her heart stuttered every time Dixon's heated gaze landed on her. Looking down at Augie, she knew her mind was made up.

She would take a chance.

Her son deserved to know his father and his side of the family. She didn't have much of a family, except for a few scattered, distant relatives. This could be her chance to give him a family who would love him.

Then there was the shifter thing.

She knew nothing of that, and it would be best for him to be around his people.

"Deja," Dixon called out. She blinked, not realizing she had been so lost in thought.

"I'm sorry. Were you talking to me?" she asked, looking at him as he walked toward her. He knelt down next to her chair.

"Yes. Percy and Mason were able to scent the lion shifters in your yard and around the neighborhood. We need to move you." Her heart pounded in her chest. Strangers had been moving around in her yard, contemplating causing harm to her and her child?

How had her life shifted to this? One moment, she was a small-town waitress raising a baby on her own, then she'd became a person of interest to a lion shifter and needed protection.

"Where?"

"For now, the lodge, with me. You'll be safest there."

Her grip tightened on August as she thought of people wanting to hurt her son. She would do whatever she needed to do to ensure that her son was safe.

"Who would want to harm a baby?" she whispered as she stared down at her precious child. She leaned down and placed a kiss on his forehead.

"A sick individual who would stop at nothing to get the power that he wants. I promise you, nothing will happen to you or August. Trust me." Dixon took her hand in his and brought it up to his lips. She closed her eyes and nodded.

"Let me go pack."

His tiger paced beneath his skin, ready to attack. Just the thought of his woman and son in danger was enough to send his tiger on the defense. A tiger protecting his mate and cub was dangerous. He stared out at the night sky. The snow had finally settled. The dark sky was clear, with a few stars lining the black backdrop.

He could hear Deja moving around in the bedroom of his hotel suite. Her moving to the hotel with him was a big step. Now, if only he could talk her into moving in with him in Cleveland. He knew he was asking much for a human. He would be patient, and once he had taken care of this issue with Tyson, he would take his time. He didn't want to scare her away.

His ringing cell phone cut through the air. He pulled it out of his jeans and looked down at the glass screen. An unknown number was calling.

The hairs on the back of his neck stood at attention. He swiped the screen to answer it.

"What?" he answered, having no patience for anything at the moment.

"Dixon."

The rage that had been festering in his gut now rose at the sound of the voice coming through his phone.

"Tyson," he growled. "What the hell do you want?"

"You know, what I will always want. Your seat on the PLC."

"It's not yours to have. You didn't earn it, nor were you—"

"I hear congratulations are in order, Dixon."

Dixon fell quiet. His tiger growled low in his chest at what Tyson was hinting at. The way the shifter spoke his name caused his hand to grip his phone tightly. He knew he needed to be careful with his strength. He had been through quite a few phones due to destroying them with his crushing strength.

He closed his eyes and took a few deep breaths. Deja and August were safely tucked away in the other room.

"I don't know what you're speaking about." He would play dumb. He didn't want to give into the lion's sneaky way of trying to find out information.

"Oh, don't play dumb, tiger. You know exactly what I'm talking about. It seems you carelessly planted your seed and it took in a little waitress. I wonder how many other bastards you have running around."

"You stay away from my family," he growled into the phone, ignoring the jab. His skin tingled from his tiger rising to the surface, begging to be let out.

"Family? Had you not gone back to that God-awful snow trap, you wouldn't even have known the waitress had bore your bastard."

Dixon growled low at the word 'bastard.' In the shifter world, marriage wasn't necessary. A mating, the joining of two souls, was much deeper than two humans signing a piece of paper, promising to be together forever. Humans divorced all the time. Two mates separating was unheard of. A mating was destined by fate.

It was forever.

Hearing August be called a bastard riled his tiger. Calling him that word would signify in the shifter world, an offspring that the father wants nothing to do with.

He would be in August's life. August was his heir.

"They are none of your concern. You want a fight? Fight me. Leave them out of this."

"Are you challenging me? Lion versus tiger?" Tyson barked out a laugh.

"To end this, I am. I'm calling you out. Tiger versus lion. I win, you leave my family alone and you stop vying for the PLC feline chair. You win, the seat is yours. You'd have all the power."

Silence greeted him. He knew what he was offering, but it was all worth it. To have his cub grow up in a safe environment was worth it. To live a life of peace would be worth it. To live a life with Deja and see her grow round with their future cubs had his tiger growling.

"You know the rules of the PLC and fighting for a seat. It's to the death. Are you sure you want to go there with me, tiger?" Tyson snarled.

Dixon thought of his future in the other room and knew that he wouldn't hesitate to keep them safe. To the death, so be it.

"My offer still stands."

"Your offer is too tempting to pass up. You're on."

The line went dead. Dixon growled and tossed his phone against the wall with such strength, it shattered into pieces.

"What did you just agree to?" Deja's soft voice appeared behind him. He turned to find her standing in the doorway in a cotton nightgown that stopped mid-thigh. Her long dark locks flowed past her shoulders. He looked into her wide eyes and felt his cock stiffen.

"Claim her," his tiger roared. He stood still as she walked over to him. He could scent the nervousness, and the slight hint of fear.

"You don't need to fear me," he snapped, angry that he would instill fear into his mate.

"It's not you that I'm afraid of." She stopped just in front of him. Her tantalizing womanly scent reached his nostrils as he looked down at her. Her clear blue eyes stared back up into his. His cock strained against his jeans, demanding to be let out. He reached out a hand and cupped her jaw. She closed her eyes and leaned into his touch.

"Then what is it? Tell me, and I'll destroy whatever you're afraid of," he growled. He refused to have his woman scared of anything. He would protect her and their child with his life.

"The future," she breathed and opened her eyes. "I'm afraid of what the future holds. I've learned so much today that my brain may explode. My mind has been screaming one thing, but I'm willing to take a leap of faith and follow what my heart is saying."

"What are they telling you?" he asked softly, bringing her flush against him. Her soft body fit his hardened one perfectly. Where he was hard and muscular, she was soft and curvy.

"My mind is telling me that there is no such thing as insta-love, and there is no such thing as fated mates."

He growled at the mention that what he felt for her wasn't real. He knew it would be hard for a human to come to accept the shifter's way of life. She would have to open her mind and heart to see what destiny had planned for both of them.

"And your heart? What is it telling you?" He leaned down and placed a chaste kiss against her lips.

"Put my trust in you. Give this thing between us a chance."

That was just what he wanted to hear.

CHAPTER TEN

She wasn't sure what he had agreed to, but she knew deep down it was something important. He was risking things she still had to learn about for her and their son. She still had so much to learn about his world, but she was willing to do it. Deep in her heart, she knew he was it for her.

She gasped as he covered her mouth with his in a crushing kiss. It was a kiss of need. She could feel that he needed her. She could hear the anguish in his voice when she stood at the door, listening to his side of the conversation with whoever he spoke to. She had a feeling it was the lion shifter.

She was safe. August was safe.

She wanted to be able to let him know that she fully trusted him. She was putting not only the life of their child's in his hands, but hers as well.

Her fingers gripped the edge of his shirt and pulled it up and over his head, breaking their kiss. A groan ripped from her throat as her fingers trailed along his well-defined pectoral muscles. Leaning forward, she ran her tongue along his flat nipple. He threaded his fingers in her hair as she ran her tongue over to the other one.

"How are you always so warm? Your body is like a furnace," she murmured as she ran her fingers down the ridges of his abdomen.

"Shifter's body temperatures run hotter than humans," he replied as her fingers went to his belt buckle. She glanced up at him as he pulled her face back to his. He kissed her deeply as she undid the belt and his jeans.

Her tongue dueled with his as she returned the hot kiss. She pushed his jeans down, freeing his jutting cock. She lowered herself to her knees in front of him.

She was captivated by his thickness, and the plump vein that lined his length. She encircled him with her hand, hearing his breath catch in his throat.

"Deja," he groaned as she licked the tip of the mushroom head. She glanced up at him from her position and felt moisture seep from between her plump folds.

She felt empowered that this strong man trembled in her hands. She slid the tip into her mouth, then widened so she could slide more of him inside. She took him as far as she could before pulling back.

His curses filled the room as she focused on bringing him pleasure. His cock slid easily between her lips as she sucked him deep into her throat. She moaned, fully aroused by her actions. She slid her hand along the long length of him in tandem with her mouth, keeping a steady rhythm. Her hand slid easily along him as her saliva coated his thickness. Her core pulsed in anticipation of feeling him stretch and fill her.

She loved the saltiness of him as a few drops of his seed escaped. She knew he was close. He gripped her hair tight in his hand as he helped guide her along his cock. He thrust deep into her throat.

"Swallow," he instructed. She eagerly followed his instructions, which elicited a deep growl from him as she increased her pace. She looked up at him and locked eyes with him. His body trembled as she tightened her grip and sucked even harder. "I don't want to release yet."

He pulled out of her mouth and dragged her into a standing position. Kicking his shoes off and removing his jeans, he pulled her over to the couch and pushed up her gown. A growl filled the air at his discovery of her naked beneath.

He bent her over the back of the couch with her legs wide. She felt the blunt tip of his cock at her entrance before he slammed home.

She cried out at the sensation of him lodged deep within her slick walls. He thrust hard and deep with each motion. He gripped her hair in his hand as he controlled every motion.

"Dixon!" she cried out, pushing back against him to meet him thrust for thrust. His taking of her was fast and hard. She could do nothing but hold onto the couch as he pounded his cock deep inside of her.

"I'm not going to last long. Touch yourself," he commanded. She didn't hesitate to slide her fingers in between her folds to her engorged clit. It was sensitive and begging for attention. She dipped her fingers into her folds where his cock entered her core, where she gathered moisture to trail along to her clitoris.

"Yes!" She groaned as she began to work her swollen bud. Her legs began to tremble as a euphoric state began to build within her. She was close to the edge. She squeezed her eyes tight as she stood on her tiptoes, her fingers tipping her over the edge. As she exploded, she screamed. She bit into a pillow to keep the whole hotel from hearing her, but it wouldn't have mattered with Dixon roaring through his own release.

His fingers bit into the sides of her hips, eliciting a burning sensation as he pumped his release deep within her core. She could feel her pussy walls milk him for everything he had. His body stilled behind her. She could feel the warmth of his release inside of her.

"Shit. Deja, are you okay?" He slid his cock from her folds. She protested, not wanting to give up the feeling of him deep within her. He pulled her up and turned her around.

She opened her eyes to find his face full of concern.

"Hmm?" she murmured, having to lean against him due to her legs feeling like jelly.

"I didn't hurt you, did I?" he asked, tipping her head back so that he could look into her eyes.

She smiled and shook her head.

Every time he touched her, her body literally exploded. If she had a lifetime of encounters like this with him, then she was signing up.

Her heart apparently knew what it was talking about.

Dixon's tiger was content. After a night of making love to Deja, he knew that she was close to making up her mind on moving in with him.

Last night, they truly felt like a family. When August woke in the middle of the night, she taught him how to change a diaper, and he even tucked her into his side as she fed his son. It was a magical moment that he would forever keep in his mind. The sight of his son getting nourishment from his mate's breast was breathtaking.

He would ensure that they would be forever protected.

She and the baby were still asleep as he let Percy into the hotel suite.

"What's going on?" Percy asked as he walked inside. He paused as he looked at Dixon and chuckled. "I take it you and Deja are good?"

Dixon tried to keep the smile from spreading across his face before he nodded. He knew his friend smelled the sex in the air. Their shifter noses could pick up the finest detail of basically anything.

"I challenged Tyson," he announced, his smile fading.

"What?"

Dixon waved his longtime friend over to the couch and took a seat across from him. He ran a shaky hand through his hair as he thought of what he was about to say.

"This has been a long time coming. Tyson stalking a woman and baby is low, even for him. It's time that I end this fight between us. We need to contact the PLC and let them know that the lions are challenging my seat."

Percy nodded and leaned forward with his elbows on his knees. "I'll call them today. The council has agreed that this matter is more important. They're leaving today."

"Thanks for handling them for me. We'll have to arrange another retreat after this situation is handled."

"Have you convinced her to go home with you? That will be the only way that she can be protected during the challenge."

"I plan to. I don't trust Tyson to fight fair. There's no way I can leave her here. For all I know, if I lose, he'll still do something to her or August. I can't have that. Plus, I still have to tell my parents about August."

"Your mother is going to shit bricks." Percy leaned back and chuckled. He was right. Amelda Blackburn had made her demands known. She wanted grandbabies. He didn't have any siblings, so the fate of their family was all on him. He thought of August's smile and knew that his son would be a great shifter one day.

His heir.

"I'm not sure she's going to want to leave here—"

"I'll go," Deja's announced from the bedroom doorway. Percy and Dixon turned to find her standing behind them. Somehow, she had snuck up on the two of them without them hearing her. She was dressed in a plush white robe that was compliments of the hotel.

"Deja." He stood from his seat as she came to him.

"You won't have to convince me. Whatever I have to do to keep Augie safe, I'll do it. I don't really have a family, just my friends, but I would love for Augie to grow up surrounded by his family."

Dixon pulled her into a warm hug. His heart slammed against his chest at the first step of completing his family. He pulled back and stared into her eyes.

"I promise you that August will be surrounded by family and friends who will love him. My mother is going to spoil him like only a grandmother can."

CHAPTER ELEVEN

Yesterday had been a whirlwind. She had called her job and quit. She had given an excuse of Augie's distant family needing her to move immediately. She would miss her friends at the bar, but it was time for her to move on.

Her goodbye to Sharon was tearful and heart-wrenching. She didn't know what she would have done without her support and love. Dixon escorted her and August to Sharon's house for her goodbye. The look on Sharon's face when she introduced Dixon as August's father brought a smile to her face.

"Well, this makes the goodbye a little better knowing that Augie will be with family," Sharon said with tears flowing down her face.

"This won't be a forever goodbye," Deja said through her tears. *"We'll come back and visit, and maybe you can even come and visit us."*

"Take care of Deja and August, young man," Sharon said to Dixon. *"They mean the world to me.*

I'm not sure where you've been this past year, but I'll let bygones be bygones, if you promise me that you will love and care for them."

"*I promise, I will do my best to care for them,*" Dixon assured her friend.

She glanced down at a sleeping August, who had remained bundled up in his blankets. She looked up as a few large men exited the SUVs and approached.

"Alpha, welcome home," one of the men greeted Dixon as they arrived at the truck. He held the back door open for them. Dixon turned and motioned for her to enter first. She settled into the seat and turned to find a baby carrier already in place next to her. She glanced back at Dixon to find a small smile on his face.

"My mother." He chuckled as he gently closed the door. She laid August in the carrier and quickly buckled him in as Dixon slid into the passenger seat, while another man got into the driver's seat.

"Deja, this is Nate. Nate, this is Deja and August." Dixon made quick introductions. Her and Nate murmured polite greetings to each other as she finished tucking August into the seat. She brushed the blanket from his face to find him looking around the vehicle.

Her body swayed as Nate drove them away from

the parked jet. Her hand shook slightly as she tucked her hair behind her ear.

"Nervous?" Dixon asked, turning to look at her. It amazed her that he could pick up on her feelings the way he did.

"A little. I can't help but think about meeting your family. What if they don't like me? I'm not like you. Will they accept Augie? Will they accept me—"

"You'll be fine. I called my mother last night and told her the news. I still think I lost my hearing in my ear from her scream," he chuckled.

She settled back in her seat and stared out the window at the scenery passing by. She had never been to this city before, and it was all new to her. She had never been this far away from Colorado. She was a nervous wreck.

Who would have ever imagined that on Christmas Eve, she would pack up her house and decide to move in with the man she'd had a one-night stand with?

She glanced back over at August and got her answer.

A short while later, Nate guided the SUV up a long winding driveway. Deja pressed her nose against the cold glass as a mansion came into view. It was a massive brick and stone home that was bigger than any house she had ever been in.

Nate brought the truck around to the front of the house, stopping in the circular driveway. Deja swallowed hard as she watched the front door open. A handsome man exited and stood on the small porch.

"It's going to be fine, Deja." Dixon turned to her. His amber eyes had a way of calming her nerves. She nodded and reached over to unbuckle the sleeping August from his seat. Dixon and Nate exited the truck. She procrastinated a little, trying to ensure that August was bundled up to prevent the chill in the cold air from hitting him. She placed a blanket over his face as she pulled him to her. She braced him against her chest as her door opened.

Dixon smiled at her and held out his hand, and she slipped hers inside of his as he guided her out of the vehicle.

"My stomach just flipped," she mumbled, pulling August up firmer against her chest. Her eyes took in the other SUVs that followed them from the airport, then looked back at the house.

She was way in over her head.

Dixon said that he was wealthy, but she never realized *how* wealthy.

By the looks of the property, they were drenched

in money. She blew out a deep breath as she thought of the clothes she had on. Jeans and a thick sweater, boots, and a warm winter coat. Nothing as fancy as the woman now standing on the porch.

Her hand gripped Dixon's as he led her to the people she assumed were his parents. The large man with his arm wrapped around the woman's shoulders was stoic, while the woman's face looked concerned.

"Don't leave me," she whispered, her voice shaking from her nerves. Her first instinct was to bolt and run in the opposite direction, but she didn't think that would get her anywhere, but it would make her more embarrassed.

"Never."

"Dixon!" the woman cried out, rushing down the stairs, throwing herself into Dixon's arms. He released Deja's hand.

"Mother," he chuckled, wrapping his arms around her. "I need you to meet someone."

Deja swallowed hard. She could feel her cheeks warming at the thought of his parents knowing about their one-night stand. She didn't want to come off as a cheap woman or a slut. As his mother pulled back and focused her amber eyes on Deja, she relaxed. There was no judgment, no animosity or anger. Just curiosity.

"Hello, dear. I'm Amelda Blackburn, Dixon's mother." The woman reached out her hand to Deja as Dixon moved to her side. Deja shifted August in her arms and shook the older woman's hand.

"I'm Deja Scarlett." August chose that exact moment to release a frustrated grunt and attempted to move the blanket from his face. They all laughed at his series of grunts, followed by sucking noises. Deja smiled down at her child and removed the blanket, just enough to reveal his face, and turned her body toward the woman. Amelda's eyes melted as she took in her grandson. She gently touched his fist and cooed at him as his identical eyes met hers. "And this is August Dixon Scarlett, who loves sucking on his fist."

"Scarlett?" The woman's eyes flashed to Dixon's.

Embarrassment flooded Deja as she glanced down at the ground.

"I didn't know Dixon's last name, ma'am," she murmured in a low voice. The memory of filling out the forms for August's birth certificate came to mind. Tears had blurred her vision as she signed it. The father's name had been left blank, and the word *unknown* as the default.

"Don't worry, Mother. It will be remedied," Dixon assured her. His eyes met Deja's and she nodded. Even if things between her and Dixon didn't work out, she would not deny her son in having his father's name. It was his heritage, and from the way that Dixon spoke, August was his heir.

"Come on in the house so we can get this baby out of the cold." Amelda waved them toward the house. Dixon reached for her and pulled her to him.

She breathed him in and felt herself calm down. She tightened her grip on August as she was led into the home.

"Everything will be okay." Dixon's lips moved against her hair.

She hoped he was right.

CHAPTER TWELVE

Dixon picked August up from the bed as Deja came from the bathroom. He didn't have to use his shifter senses to tell that she was nervous as hell. Her wide eyes, and the way she wrung her hands together was all the signs he needed.

He moved to her to try to calm her. He didn't want her to feel over her head and leave. He needed her and August in his life. He should have warned his mother about August not having their last name.

The look of horror and embarrassment on Deja's face was like a punch to the stomach. He didn't fault her at all though. They hadn't even known each other's last names. A year ago, after he coaxed her into a walk after work, it led to his hotel room and the rest, as they say, was history. When he had awoken, she was gone.

"You're doing fine," he murmured, pulling her into his side.

"I'm so embarrassed. How do I explain to your parents our relationship?" She pulled her head back from him and sighed.

"Look, in our world, it's much different than humans. Shifters have what you call one-night stands all the time. It's the norm. I think she was more taken back that August doesn't have my last name."

She glanced down at August, who had snuggled himself against Dixon's chest.

"Okay."

"Now, let's go down to talk with them. I'm sure they want to get to know you and August."

She nodded her head and reached for his hand. He pulled her behind him as he left the room. He had promised to meet his parents in the solarium of the house.

Dixon led Deja through the house. He knew Blackburn Manor was in an uproar as word had spread about August's arrival. He cradled his son to his chest, loving the feel of him. His thoughts turned to the challenge that would come between him and Tyson. He tightened his grip and knew that he would do what he must to keep August safe.

They arrived at the solarium, where he guided

Deja through the open French doors before following behind her. His parents were already waiting for him. His father stood by the windows, staring out into the garden, while his mother paced the room.

"Mother. Father," he greeted his parents. His mother immediately flew across the room and stopped in front of him. He could see in her eyes that she was dying to hold August.

"May I?" she asked, looking to Deja, who nodded, giving Amelda permission.

Amelda gently took August from his arms and cradled her to him. August stretched and opened his eyes, staring up at his grandmother. She leaned down and smelled August's hair, and Dixon knew that she would smell his scent, confirming that he was indeed a Blackburn. Pure love beamed from her eyes as she glanced once more down at her grandson.

"Maxwell, would you look at him? He's perfect," she murmured, tears filling her eyes as she looked to Dixon's father. She walked over to her husband and they both smiled down at August, who laughed and cooed at them, melting both of them.

"He'll have them wrapped around his finger in no time," he murmured, pulling Deja to his side. His heart was filled with pride as his father looked up from the baby and stared across the room at him. His father, a man of few words, nodded his head to Dixon.

He gave his approval.

Dixon led Deja over to the couch as his parents turned to them. His mother took a seat in a plush chair, while his father remained by the window.

"I heard you offered a challenge to Tyson," Maxwell stated. The elder Blackburn's face was stoic as he looked to Dixon.

"Yes, I have. It's the only way that I know of to keep Deja and August safe," he admitted.

"But Dixon, you know the rules that the PLC will insist on," Amelda gasped, turning her wide gaze to him.

"Yes, I know, Mother."

"Wait. What's going on?" Deja's body stiffened beside him. She pulled away from him and turned to face him. "Isn't it just a fight?"

He stared at her, unsure of how to answer. In the shifter world, life was archaic compared to the way that humans solved problems. According to the PLC, any challenge for power would be a fight to the death.

"It's a little more than a fight." He grabbed her

hand and stared into her eyes. Everything he owned would go to her and August, should he be defeated.

"You're scaring me," she whispered, her eyes flickering to his parents before returning to him.

"The fight would be to the death."

"No! Are you crazy? There has to be another way!" She scrambled from the chair and ran a shaky hand through her hair as she looked around the room.

"You know about this?" she demanded from his parents.

"It is the way of the shifters," Amelda said softly, keeping her voice low.

"It's so barbaric!" Deja exclaimed, her eyes wide in desperation.

He stood slowly from his seat and reached for her. A sob ripped from her chest as she allowed him to wrap his arms around her.

"It will be okay. I won't lose," he murmured, holding her tight to him as her body shook from her sobs. He looked over her shoulder and met the misty eyes of his mother. She held the baby tight as she glanced up at his father, who had yet to take his eyes off of Dixon. "Even if I do fall, my parents will be there for you and August."

"But we just found each other again. I don't want to chance him growing up without a father."

A deep pain blossomed in his chest at the thought of falling to the likes of Tyson and leaving this child to grow up without him.

"He's right, my dear," Maxwell announced, coming to stand next to Dixon and Deja. "It may seem barbaric to you, but our animals are still animals, and when there is a challenge, the alpha in us will come out. My son is a strong fighter and will handle Tyson."

Deja leaned back and looked at his father. She nodded her head at the older Blackburn.

"Let's relax and try not to think about the fight. Tomorrow is Christmas. Let's enjoy the holiday before thinking of the challenge. The PLC will be calling soon to schedule it." Amelda laid a kiss on August's head. "Tomorrow is August's first Christmas. Let's make it a special one."

"I feel bad. I don't have any gifts for your parents," Deja whispered as they left the dining room.

It was Christmas morning, and they had just

finished having a wonderful breakfast with Dixon's parents. Her eyes still felt gritty from crying last night. She wasn't sure why, but the magnitude of the challenge hit her. There was a chance that Dixon would not be coming back to her.

It just wasn't fair.

She understood she was human and that the shifter's way of life was different. Now that she had Dixon, the thought of him being ripped from her and August's life had gotten to her.

"Don't be. You've just given them the best gift of all," he murmured, carrying August against his chest. His hand gripped hers as he led her into the family room, where a massive, decorated tree sat off in the corner. The smell of the crisp Douglas fir filled the air.

Her eyes locked onto the tree, finding it to be one of the most beautifully decorated trees she had ever seen. It had to have stood ten feet tall, and didn't even come near the tall vaulted ceilings. She smiled as she turned, and found August's eyes captivated by the Christmas lights.

"You see the pretty lights?" she murmured, running her hand along his back. Her eyes flickered to Dixon and found his on her.

"There's a present underneath the tree for you," he announced, his lips tilted up in the corners.

"Dixon, I didn't—"

"Stop. It doesn't matter. I want for nothing, and this little guy is all the gift that I need," he chuckled as August squealed. She laughed as her son smiled at his father.

Her heart rate spiked, as if she were a child on Christmas morning. She smiled and raced over to the tree, jumping around in excitement. A flat box wrapped in red paper called to her. She leaned down and grabbed the box. Finding her name on it, she scooped it up and headed toward the couch to sit down.

Dixon chuckled as she bounced in the seat. Her fingers paused on the gift as she looked over at Dixon.

"Dixon, you just couldn't wait to open the gifts, could you?" Amelda's voice appeared as she and Maxwell came into the room. "Even as a child, this boy would wake us up at the crack of dawn to get to his gifts."

Deja laughed at the thought of a young Dixon waking his parents up in excitement.

"The boy never did understand the value of

getting rest," Maxwell murmured as he took a seat in the large recliner.

"Well, I'm sure we'll have plenty more Christmases where August will be the one waking his mother and me up to get to his presents."

Deja bit her lip at the thought of waking up with Dixon in the future.

"Go ahead, Deja. Open your gift." Dixon nodded as he moved toward her. She glanced back to the gift, feeling all eyes in the room on her.

She ripped open the box and found a stack of papers in it. She looked up at Dixon, confused, but his face didn't change. He nodded for her to take a look at them.

Picking them up, she began to read. She gasped as her eyes flew across the pages.

"Dixon!" He kneeled in front of her with their child. His parents remained silent as they watched the exchange between them. "What is this?"

"If I should fall, you and August will be taken care of. Everything I own is yours. Neither of you will ever want for anything."

Her eyes burned as tears filled them. She tried her best to hold them back because she knew if they fell, she wouldn't be able to stop them. Money didn't matter to her, *he* mattered to her. Her heart would shatter without Dixon in her life. In just a short period of time, she had fallen for him.

"But you will win. You will come back to me." Her voice strengthened with conviction as she stared into his eyes. She believed it in her heart that fate couldn't be so cruel as to finally complete their family, only to take Dixon away from her and August. She reached out a hand to him, connecting with the scruff on his jawline. She smiled through her tears as she searched his gaze. "August will need his father. I will need you."

CHAPTER THIRTEEN

Dixon growled as he tore Deja's clothes off. His need for her mounted as his tiger paced beneath his skin. After leaving August with his mother, he practically carried Deja to his suite. His tiger demanded that he claim her now. There was no fighting it anymore.

"Dixon!" Deja cried out as he picked her naked form up and tossed her onto his bed. He rid himself of his clothing as he took in her perfect body lying across his bed. A growl rumbled deep within his chest as his eyes took in her body. Her dark areolas called to him. He ached to taste her sweet skin. His eyes trailed their way down to take in her soft belly. This was where his son had grown, was nourished and protected until the day he was born. His tiger wanted to lay claim to her and fill her with his seed.

"Plant another heir inside of her."

Next time he would be there. He would not miss the birth of their next child. This was a promise that he made to himself and his future.

He slowly crawled onto the bed. His eyes locked onto hers as he made his way over her. Her legs fell apart, inviting him to settle against her slick core. The smell of her arousal filled the air, announcing that she was ready for him. He braced himself over her as she returned his hot gaze.

"Deja."

"Make me yours, Dixon. Claim me," she murmured. She threaded her fingers into the hair at the base of his neck as she guided his face to hers. He crushed his mouth to hers in a bruising kiss. Her tongue met his, coaxing it into her mouth. The taste of her burst onto his tongue as he kissed her with everything he had.

His thick cock brushed her slick opening as she thrust her hips against him. It demanded entrance into her. It was ready to plunge deep inside of her.

"Please, Dixon. Do it," she gasped, tearing her lips from his. Her eyes met his and he knew that she would forever be his.

He felt his incisors break free from his gums. He shifted his hips and surged forward, thrusting his cock deep within her drenched core.

Her walls gripped him tight as he paused to allow her to get accustomed to his size. Deja threw her head back in ecstasy as she cried out. She was tight, but slick, and he knew that she would be ready for him. He pulled back and thrust again, repeating the motion, plunging deep. His eyes locked on the curve of her neck.

Bite her, a voice whispered in the back of his mind.

"Deja." Her name was ripped from his throat in a guttural groan as she met him thrust for thrust. She turned her head away and his tiger roared.

His jaws widened as he sank his fangs into her shoulder, eliciting a scream from her. A shifter's bite during sex triggered an orgasmic response, sending her over the brink into an intense release. Her walls gripped him as he released her shoulder from his mouth. He pulled back and roared as she milked his release from him. The taste of her blood coated his tongue, and it was a taste that would be burned on his tongue forever.

Deja Scarlett belonged to him.

He exploded.

He thrust deep as he filled her with his seed. His body shook as his orgasm poured over him. He trembled as he continued to thrust, his beast trying to plant his seed to create another bond between the two of them, to ensure the future of his name.

His hips slowed as he settled in the valley of Deja's hips. He gasped for breath, trying to will his heart to settle. He glanced down at his mark on her shoulder and found blood seeping from the wound. He licked it. The enzymes in his saliva would heal the wound, but leave his mark on her.

She was his.

Forever.

Her breaths began to slow down. No words were needed between them as he cleaned her shoulder. He felt her love for him and he wanted to return the feeling. He would win the fight. He refused to fall to the likes of Tyson. His stake in the challenge was far more than Tyson's would ever be.

They remained joined, his cock nestled deep within her. She turned her face to his, her eyes filled with tears.

"Did I hurt you?" he asked, scared for a second that his bite caused her pain. She shook her head as she returned his gaze.

"Don't leave me," she whispered, reaching up with her hand and cupping his jaw. "I love you, Dixon August Blackburn. Don't make me raise our son by myself."

His heart stuttered at her admission. He searched her eyes and knew that she spoke the truth.

"I love you, Deja Scarlett. I will never leave you." He bent down and brushed his lips against hers. He pulled back and slowly traced his mark with his fingertips. "This is symbolic of my love for you. In my world, this shows that you are the other half of my soul. My heart. Any shifter who sees it will know that with one look, one smell."

"How can I mark you? To put my claim on you?" she whispered, a lone tear falling from her eye. He watched as it left a trail along her skin, before disappearing into her dark hair.

"A shifter heals fast. Even if you bit me, my skin would heal the mark. But there is a way. There is a special tattoo that can be embedded into my skin that will show I am a mated man. Besides your scent being all over me, we can do the tattoo if you want."

She nodded her head as he bent his to hers, needing another kiss. He'd be willing to do whatever she wanted to please her. Tattooing his skin to signify he belonged to her pleased his tiger. It liked the fact that their mate wanted to lay claim to them. Her soft lips moved across his as the kiss began to deepen. His buried cock began to swell.

"Again?" she gasped, breaking the kiss. He

smiled down at her, brushing her hair from her face. She would need to know that tiger shifters could go for hours when mating. A year ago, their night together was filled with all night sex. That would never change. He wanted her in a way that his body would always crave. She was the perfect woman for him, made just for him.

"I'll always want you," he growled, pulling back and thrusting deep. The scent coming from her drove his tiger wild. His tiger wanted to fill her with their seed again.

It was determined to secure their future.

The distant sound of a phone ringing filled the air. Deja groaned as she turned over in the bed. She opened her eyes and found herself faced with the muscular chest of Dixon. He reached over her and grabbed his blaring phone from the nightstand.

Their entire day had been filled with frantic lovemaking. The soreness between her legs caused a smile to spread across her lips. Just the memories of Dixon taking her in so many different positions throughout the day caused her heart to race. She had never been taken before with such passion. His loving was almost desperate, and he had taken such care of her to ensure she had climaxed every time. She didn't know how he did it. Every time she thought he'd had his fill of her, she would feel his long length stiffen again.

She licked her lips, remembering the salty taste of his release in her mouth. She had taken advantage of him as well, needing to get her fill of him too. There wasn't a place on her body that his cock hadn't entered. She shivered, thinking of him pushing into her from behind. It had been the first time that anyone had entered her forbidden hole. He had taken great care of her, and it left her craving him to take her there again. Just the thought of how hard her orgasm was had her legs clamping together.

Deja tried to block out what they were facing. She knew the moment would come when he would get the call.

She glanced over to the windows as Dixon moved to sit on the edge of the bed as he spoke to someone on the phone. Night had fallen, and August was resting in the adjoining room.

A small cry filled the air. She moved from the bed, wrapping herself in the top sheet in a toga fashion. She hurried to the other room and smiled as he began to fuss. She scooped him up from his bed and cradled him in her arms, resting her lips against his head as she moved him to the changing table.

Dixon hadn't lied when he said his mother would spoil August. Within a day, she had already turned the adjoining room into a nursery for her grandchild. Deja quickly finished changing her fussy baby.

"I know what you want," she cooed to him as she picked him up and walked back into Dixon's— *their* bedroom. She smiled at the notion that they officially belonged to each other.

The tone of Dixon's voice changed as he spoke. Worry filled her as she got on the bed and leaned back against the plush pillows. August's cries grew louder as his face thrust back and forth on her covered breast. She untucked the sheet from around her and revealed her bare breast to her son. He didn't need any help latching onto her.

"They couldn't wait another week or two?" Dixon growled into the phone. A shiver passed through her as the anger rolled off her mate. Just the sound of the word in her mind made her core clench.

Dixon belonged to her.

And here he was on the phone, discussing the

challenge. Something that could take him from her.

"Fine." He disconnected the call and leaned forward, bracing his elbows on his knees. He ran a shaky hand through his hair.

"When?" she asked quietly. She dreaded the answer. Looking back down at their son, she watched as he settled down and fed. She brushed his dark hair that was identical to Dixon's. She felt the bed dip as Dixon moved to her side. He tucked her against him as they watched August at her breast.

"Tomorrow."

She closed her eyes and willed herself not to cry. She would remain strong for Dixon and August. She opened her eyes and nodded, not trusting herself to speak. Instead, she basked in the feel of her man at her side and her baby at her breast.

CHAPTER FOURTEEN

Dixon's tiger was on edge. The challenge would commence soon. According to the PLC, they could not stall on the challenge. Once the challenge had been issued and accepted, it had to take place as soon as possible after notification to the PLC. Percy walked alongside him as they made their way through the woods to the meeting point. His family walked behind him in support. The ground, covered in a small amount of snow, would be unforgiving in a fight.

Deja, who refused to remain back at the mansion, walked alongside his mother. She demanded to be at the challenge, insisting that if she were to be a part of his world that she would have to be there. The stubborn tilt of her head let him know that he had lost their first argument. The heated kiss they shared was not one of goodbye, but one of future and love.

They came to a clearing that housed quite a few people. Representatives of the Paranormal League Committee would be present to ensure that the challenge was fair, and that there would be no interference. Interfering in the middle of a challenge for a seat on the PLC would be immediate disqualification, and those caught interfering could be punished by death.

"You will defeat Tyson," Percy muttered to him with a slap on his back as they came to a halt.

Tyson stood on the other side of the clearing. A cocky smile filled the lion shifter's face as he returned Dixon's glare. Dixon channeled his anger toward the shifter. Tyson's lion would be no match for Dixon's tiger.

"Greetings, Dixon Blackburn," Lador called out. The alpha of the bears approached Dixon with a grim look on his face. Dixon gripped the large man's hand in a firm shake.

"Lador," Dixon murmured, feeling his tiger too close to the surface. It could sense danger near and was unsettled. It slammed against his chest as it demanded to be let out. His eyes locked onto Tyson's across the clearing as Lador greeted his family. He broke the glare as he looked around the clearing, taking in the tiger shifters that were present to show their support.

Losing to Tyson would not just affect his family, but all tiger shifters. Tigers had represented the feline shifters for decades, and they all depended on him to maintain his seat on the council.

"Dixon, please follow me." Lador's voice grabbed his attention. He nodded and followed behind the mountain of a man. Bear shifters tended to be on the larger side. Lador towered over Dixon by at least a few inches. Caesar, the alpha of the wolves, escorted Tyson to the center of the clearing.

The air grew tense as he locked glares with the lion shifter once more.

"I see you brought the whole family to see you die today," Tyson growled. "You sure you want your woman and cub to see you die?"

"I won't be dying today," Dixon growled, refusing to fall for Tyson's taunts. His tiger paced, knowing he would be free soon.

"Now you two know the rules of a challenge," Lador announced, standing next to them. Members of the PLC surrounded the two shifters. Viktor, the

Master Vampire, Ratha, Queen of the Fae, Xena, the Grand Priestess of the Witches, all stood around them, representing the PLC. They would bear witness to the fight for who would sit in the feline shifter chair after today. "You will shift into your animals. The animal standing at the end of the fight will have the feline shifter chair. Is that understood?"

Dixon nodded, keeping all expressions at bay as he faced Tyson. He turned and walked back toward Percy.

"That asshole is too fucking cocky," Percy announced as he reached his side.

"I'm going to enjoy erasing that smile from his face." Dixon began to strip his clothes off. His animal let loose a deep growl, causing his chest to rumble. "If anyone tries to interfere—"

"You don't have to say a word." Percy's serious eyes met his. Dixon knew that his best friend would have his back.

"If I should fall—"

"Stop." Percy held up a hand and shook his head. Dixon knew he didn't have to ask. Deja and August would be taken care of.

"Dixon!" Deja jogged over to him. His eyes greedily took her in as her dark hair flowed around her shoulders. She held their son against her chest in a contraption that was strapped around her body. Her eyes were wide as she stopped in front of him.

"Deja. You and August would be safer with my parents," he murmured, reaching for her. He leaned down and placed a lingering kiss against her lips. He pulled back and trailed his hand along August's head, which was covered by a tiny winter hat. He laid a gentle kiss on the baby's head. He paused and breathed in deeply, taking the scent of his son with him.

"I just wanted to say that I don't like the looks of that Tyson character. Kick his ass," she hissed between her teeth. He smiled, loving that his little sex kitten had claws. He smiled and placed another kiss on her lips.

"I plan to." He pulled back from her and turned her away from him. He gave her a gentle push in the direction of his father before meeting the elder Blackburn's eyes. His father nodded to him.

It wasn't much, but he got his father's message loud and clear.

End the lion.

He returned his father's nod as he watched Deja return to the safety of his parent's side.

"Let's get this shit over with," Dixon muttered as he turned his back to his family. His fangs descended from his gums as the change took him. He fell to the ground as his bones crackled and reformed. His orange and black fur burst forward as his animal finally broke free. His vision sharpened as he focused on the lion that stood in the clearing.

His tiger roared as it planted its massive paws apart. He narrowed his eyes on the lion as it too let loose a roar. The air stilled as the two animals stalked toward each other. The scent of his mate and child remained lodged in his nostrils.

It was time to end this game with Tyson. He had a promise to keep.

Deja refused to look away. She would forever remember this day. It would be burned into her memory. She watched with baited breath as Dixon's tiger wrestled Tyson's lion on the ground. Amelda's arms wrapped around her as she held August tight to her chest.

The lion roared as Dixon's teeth sank into his shoulder. He flung Dixon off and pounced on top him.

"Dixon," she whispered as tears flowed down her face, taking in the battle of lion versus tiger. Amelda squeezed her tighter.

She glanced over at Dixon's mother and took notice of the tears that flowed down her cheeks too. It couldn't be easy for her to watch her son go through something as brutal as this, not knowing if he would make it through the challenge.

Dixon's tiger let out a series of growls as he used his hind legs to kick free from Tyson's grip. The two shifters circled each other. Dixon swiped at Tyson with is large paw, missing the lion. He ducked and skidded away from Tyson as he dove at him.

Dixon swiped another paw at him, his massive fangs on display.

"Stop playing with him," Maxwell growled beside her. She turned to Dixon's father to find his eyes locked on the fight. His face was drawn tight as he watched his only son fight for his life.

She turned her eyes back to the fight and willed Dixon to win. She refused to think of any other option for this fight to come to an end. She watched as the members of the PLC stood around the circle to ensure that no one could cross the imaginary line. She took in the other people who stood back, witnessing the fight. From what Dixon had explained, other shifters would come to witness the challenge.

A loud roar filled the air. Her eyes flew to the fight that was a blur of paws, fangs, and tails as the two battled. Her breath caught in her throat as she watched Tyson land on top of Dixon. She feverishly brushed the tears from her eyes as her heart slammed against her chest.

"No!" The one word tore from her as she watched Dixon make every attempt at getting Tyson off him. She unconsciously took a step toward him, but was pulled back by Amelda. Her eyes took in the blood that marred the pristine white snow that covered the ground.

"He'll get up. My son will get up," Amelda whispered fiercely, squeezing her tight. "He is a strong tiger."

She breathed a sigh of relief as she watched him flip the both of them over. His massive fangs sank deep into the lion's neck. The lion released a roar as he tried to shake off the tiger, but the massive orange beast didn't let up on the lion. He planted his feet on the lion's chest and shook its massive head, shredding the lion's neck.

Silence surrounded them as everyone waited to

see if the lion would get up. Dixon pulled back his head and let out a roar that echoed for miles around. His massive tiger head turned to her, and she could see the bloodstained fur around his mouth. He stepped away from the still lion and paced back and forth near the body.

She moved to run to Dixon again, but Amelda held onto her.

"Not yet," she murmured, relief evident in her voice as her eyes remained on that of her son as he paced.

They all watched as the large man named Lador marched over to the lion and bent down to assess it.

Deja began unsnapping the baby carrier that held August to her. She handed August to Amelda, who cradled the baby to her chest.

Deja's heart raced as she waited for the man to make an announcement. She bit her lip as the large man straightened to his full height.

"Dixon Blackburn, the seat remains yours."

The crowd watching the battle roared. Those that supported the lion shifter protested, while those in favor of Dixon celebrated. She had never been so happy for someone to die before, but when it came to a stranger who wanted to do harm to her and her child and the man that she loved, she would always side with killing the enemy.

"Dixon," she murmured, taking a single step forward.

She watched as he let loose another roar, asserting himself as the victor. The lion's body began to shimmer, and as she watched, his body began to morph back into that of his human self. The mangled body of the shifter lied lifeless in the bloodied snow.

Dixon turned his head and his eyes locked onto hers. Her feet took another step forward as her eyes remained on Dixon. She watched as the air around him began to shimmer and ran to him as he stood in his naked, human body.

He didn't take his eyes off her as he moved toward her, brushing past people who were trying to congratulate him. His body was covered in bruises and blood, but she didn't care. He was the most beautiful thing she had ever laid her eyes on.

"Dixon!" He drew her in as she threw herself at him. She was sobbing as she wrapped her arms and legs around him. She chanted his name as he held her tight.

"I told you I would never leave you," he murmured in her ear. She pulled away to look at him through her tear-filled eyes. She smiled at him, her heart full with love for this man in front of her.

"Don't ever scare me like that again," she warned, leaning forward and pressing her lips to his.

"We have a lifetime to look forward to together, and believe me, scaring you is the last thing I plan to do to you."

EPILOGUE

Eight Months Later

Deja smiled as she followed behind Dixon and August. Dixon jogged along in front of her with August sitting on his shoulders.

"Come on, slow poke!" Dixon called out, turning around. She laughed as she took in August letting loose a toothy scream. His face lit up as he saw her waddling behind them.

They had done it again.

Dixon had knocked her up again on Christmas.

She was starting to see a pattern with them, only this time, there was a slight difference. This was the second gift he had bestowed upon her on Christmas day. She rubbed her large belly and grimaced as she tried to increase her speed. Gone were the days that she could see her feet.

"I can only go so fast," she called out. She loved to see her boys together. Dixon was an amazing father, and she couldn't have asked for anyone better to spend the rest of her life with.

She adjusted her sunglasses on her face as she continued. The Blackburn's had taken grandparenting to a new level. They had build a small playground on the family grounds. Not only was there a playground for August for when he could walk, but a play area for when he shifted and could play as a tiger cub. She couldn't wait to see her baby when he shifted. From what she had learned, cubs usually shifted for the first time between four to five years old.

By the time she had caught up with the two men in her life, Dixon had placed August in the baby swing and had him laughing. The beautiful sounds of her son's laughter made her heart pound.

"Hey, handsome," she greeted as she arrived at Dixon's side. She tilted her head back and offered her lips to him. He bent down and brushed his lips across hers.

"How's my mate holding up?" His eyes latched onto her belly.

For this pregnancy, he had gotten to be there every step of the way, not missing one part. He had insisted on not knowing the sex of the baby. He claimed it didn't matter to him, but Deja knew. She was hoping for a girl to even the family out.

"We're doing okay," she murmured, pulling back from him. She smiled at August as he reached for her. She blew him a kiss, which caused him to laugh again.

"Are you sure you don't want to know the sex?" she asked as Dixon pushed August. She had kept the secret for a few months now, and was dying to share it with him.

"Nope. I can be patient. We don't have much longer."

Deja huffed and put her hand on her hips. "This is the hardest secret I've ever had to keep."

Dixon glanced her way with his eyebrow cocked.

"Okay. Maybe second hardest secret." She laughed as she pushed her hair behind her ear.

"I can wait."

"Don't you at least want to know how many?"

His eyes flew to hers in shock. She could visibly see him swallow. His mouth moved, but no words came out.

"How many?" he finally asked. If she didn't know any better, she would say his face grew pale.

She smiled and held up two fingers.

Twins.

She guessed her tiger was trying to outdo himself by planting two little gifts in her womb last Christmas.

"Come here," he whispered, reaching for her. She didn't hesitate as she moved into his arms. "I love you," he murmured.

"I love you too."

Everything was right in her life. She couldn't wait to meet these two little gifts from her tiger. She just wouldn't tell him that they would have to try again after this pregnancy for her little girl.

The End

A LETTER TO THE READER

Dear Reader,

Thank you for taking the time to read A Tiger's Gift! I hope that you enjoyed reading their story as much as I enjoyed writing it. Please feel free to leave a review to let me know your thoughts. I love reading reviews from my readers. Even if you didn't like it, I would love to know why. Reviews can be left on the platform you purchased the book, and even Goodreads!

Make sure you will explore one of the other books I have available!

Love,

Ariel Marie

HER WARRIOR DRAGON

Sneak Peek

He closed his eyes briefly as he glided higher into the sky. His massive wingspan allowed him to pierce through the dense clouds as his elevation increased. Vander blew out a snort, as his dragon was in full-blown battle mode, ready for combat. He loved the exhilarating feeling of gliding through the air, allowing his dragon to be in control. But, tonight would not be a night of pleasurable flight.

He was on the hunt for one black dragon that had attempted to annihilate an entire farming village.

Gamair, the Death Lord, was a dragon who was pure evil, obsessed with death. Vander, The Warrior, was a dragon shifter, and one who would put a stop to the evil monster. He would not allow the Death Lord to wreak havoc on entire communities of innocent people, all because the black dragon had nothing better to do. Vander had fought Gamair for centuries, and knew most of the black dragon's tricks, but this time, he had gone too far.

Dragons had long been champions of the human race, but rarely revealed themselves to the world. When they did, they used their magic to distort the human mind. To humans, dragons were a myth, a legend.

Tonight's battle of dragons would be distorted to any human that would happen to look up and see the massive creatures in the clouds.

His dragon sensed two large presences in the sky near him. He glanced around and found Jodos, his best friend since childhood, gliding next to him, while his older brother, Feno, swooped in to his right, flying alongside him. Gamair would not stand a chance on this night.

Vander turned his attention back toward the sky, only to realize he'd lost sight of Gamair. His keen eyes searched the dense clouds, but there was no sign of the black dragon.

"There!" Feno's voice broke through telepathically. Vander looked in the direction of his brother's

stare, and he could see the tail of the black dragon, but it disappeared again in the midst of the dense clouds.

"I'm going up higher," Vander informed Jodos and Feno.

He couldn't afford to let Gamair get away. He pumped his wings, gaining momentum as he went higher into the sky, intent on finding the dragon and taking him out. If they didn't stop him soon, he would destroy more lives, and Vander would be damned if he would let that happen.

Gamair came into view, and Vander's dragon didn't hesitate. He opened his large mouth and breathed fire. Flames danced along Gamair's scales as he flew closer. The black dragon flipped out of the path of Vander's flames, and threw a massive white ball of power toward him.

He tried to dodge the attack, but the energy hit Vander square in his dragon's chest. The energy paralyzed him, leaving his dragon unable to pump his wings. Both man and dragon panicked. The wind blew past his face as his body began to head toward the ground. He felt himself lose control over his dragon.

The sound of his brother's voice yelling his name filled his head, but he was unable to respond as he fell through the clouds. He knew that he was in trouble when he felt the shift begin.

You have got to be fucking kidding me, he thought as his human arms appeared. His dragon left, and his full human body came forward. He blinked his eyes and let loose a curse at the speed in which he was falling.

"This is going to hurt," he muttered as the ground rushed up, then everything went black.

Faye looked at the clock and groaned. She had six more hours until the end of her twelve-hour shift. The life of an emergency room nurse was rewarding, but taxing on her body. Tonight was her fourth night in a row. She had picked up some extra shifts, trying to earn extra money to pay down her student loans.

Six more months of double payments and they would be paid off. Financial freedom was her goal, and she was almost there, so this sacrifice would be well worth it. Just the thought of being free of major debt put a little more pep in her step.

She was transporting a patient who came into

the ER with chest pain. His tests came back abnormal, so she had to escort him to the cath lab so that the interventional cardiologist could do an invasive test to check for blockages in the arteries surrounding his heart.

He wouldn't be coming back to the ER. He'd either go to the cardiac floor to be admitted, or the operating room, if what they found it warranted an emergency surgery.

"Okay, here we go, Mr. Sullivan," she said as she opened the doors for Mike, the nursing assistant. She quickly followed behind and reached the side of the cart. The sounds of his heartbeat on the machines echoed down the narrow hallway.

"Thank you, Faye," Mr. Sullivan said, reaching out for her hand. He was an older gentleman in his late sixties, with salt and pepper hair, and a warm smile. The entire night, he hadn't complained, not once. It was his wife who had insisted he come to the emergency room when he had argued it was only heartburn. "I appreciate everything you've done for me."

"Oh, it's not a problem," she replied, squeezing his hand. This was why she became a nurse. Sometimes, patients just needed a comforting hand and a smile to help get them through the scary times. "I just want to make sure that you're good enough to get back to that pretty wife of yours," she added with a smile.

"I mean it. Don't you stop smiling," he said as Mike wheeled him into the lab where the team of nurses and physicians were waiting.

"I won't. Now, I'm leaving you in good hands." They quickly grabbed the monitor and exited the room with a wave so that the team could proceed with the procedure.

"What are you doing this weekend?" Mike asked, holding the door open for her.

"After I wake from my work-induced coma, I may go out with my friend, Jenna, this weekend. She's wanted to go to this bar she heard about. You and Nina have any plans?"

"I have no clue what she's planning, but me? My focus will be on the playoffs this weekend." He laughed.

Faye rolled her eyes at her coworker. She knew that Mike's wife would be dragging him out to wherever she wanted to go this weekend. They made their way back to the emergency department and found everything calm. She enjoyed working with this team. Everyone was professional, and worked together well.

"Hey, Faye!" her charge nurse, Tim, called out from the nurse's station. "You're up for the next trauma."

"Sure thing, Boss." She walked over to the nurse's station and leaned against the counter. "Just let all emergency calls know that they can only come after I grab a bite to eat and get my coffee," she joked. She batted away the balled up paper Tim tossed at her.

"Sure thing. I'll let all the squads know that Faye needs a diversion until after her break," Tim said as he stood.

"I knew you were my favorite charge nurse," she said in a singsong voice. She turned away from the counter and headed toward the break room.

The smell of freshly brewed coffee greeted her as she pushed the door open.

"Somebody loves me," she exclaimed, making a beeline straight for the coffee pot.

Faye grabbed her cup from the dish rack by the sink and moved the carafe out of the way before sliding her mug beneath the flow of beautiful, black, liquid gold. Coffee was a nurse's secret weapon to surviving the evening shift. Once her cup was filled, she grabbed her flavored creamer from the fridge and doctored her coffee to perfection. Who needed food when they had this liquid perfection?

Her lunch was forgotten as she grabbed the remote for the TV and sat at the table, putting her feet up. It was Friday night in Blue Creek, and so far, nothing much was going on. Hopefully, she could make it through the rest of her shift without any action.

In a town like Blue Creek, where there was a healthy mixture of the supernatural population, one never knew when things would jump off. But, tonight, she would keep her fingers crossed and pray there was no action.

"Level one trauma!" The operator's voice came through the overhead speaker. Faye groaned. Quickly taking a healthy sip of her coffee, she paused to listen. "ETA, five minutes."

"Shit!" she exclaimed, her feet hitting the floor as she jumped up. Hating to waste any coffee, she tried to gulp as much as she could down, but it burned the crap out of her mouth. She tossed the coffee into the sink and placed her mug on the counter.

"All I know is this person better be dying," she muttered as she rushed out of the break room.

ABOUT THE AUTHOR

Ariel Marie is an author who loves the paranormal, action and hot steamy romance. She combines all three in each and every one of her stories. For as long as she can remember, she has loved vampires, shifters and every creature you can think of. This even rolls over into her favorite movies. She loves a good action packed thriller! Throw a touch of the supernatural world in it and she's hooked!

Ariel puts this together to give her readers updates! Her subscribers are usually one of the first to learn about her releases, ARC signups and giveaways!

Sign up for Ariel Marie's Newsletter

ALSO BY THE AUTHOR

An Erotic Vampire Series

Vampire Destiny

The Dark Shadows Series

Princess

Toma

Phaelyn

Teague

Adrian

Nicu

The Mirrored Prophecy Series

Power of the Fae

Fight for the Fae

Future of the Fae (TBD)

The Dragon Curse Series (Ménage MFF Erotic Series)

Mating Two Dragons

Loving Two Dragons

Claiming Two Dragons

Taking Two Dragons (Feb. 2018)

Sassy Ever After Kindle World

Her Warrior Dragon

Her Fierce Dragon (Feb. 2018)

Her Guardian Dragon (TBD)

Stand Alone Book

Dani's Return

A Faery's Kiss

Fourteen Shades of F*cked Up: An Anthology

Tiger Haven

Searching For His Mate

12 Magical Nights of Christmas Anthology

Sin & Seduction Box Set (Coming Feb. 2018)

Printed in Great Britain
by Amazon